SOMETHI[NG] TO COME OVER THE GIRL.
HER FACE DRAINED OF COLOR
AND SHE WOBBLED SLIGHTLY
IN HER HARD-BACKED CHAIR.

She fell, like a wilting rosebud, slightly sideways, soon destined for the floor but for Ransom's quick reflexes. He caught her neatly, ignoring the surprised whispers behind him, and pressed the back of his hand to her forehead as he lowered her gently to the wooden floor. Then he slid two fingers past her *kapp* string and felt for the pulse in her soft neck; he found it strong and steady. "Fainted only," he pronounced quietly, thinking that Bishop Umble would probably continue with the ceremony whether one girl fainted or ten.

"She needs to eat," Ransom commanded softly over his shoulder to an elderly woman, aware that the girl had been most likely too focused on her duties as attendant to eat any breakfast. It took a few moments, but then someone passed forward a small glass of water and a morsel in a white cloth napkin. *Gut*, he thought. Water first. He coaxed it between her lips, and her eyelids fluttered. Then he checked in the napkin. Great. *Pie.* He pressed some crumbs to her lips and she opened her wide blue eyes in both dawning surprise and dismay.

"I've ruined my best friend's wedding."

Also by Kelly Long

The Amish Bride of Ice Mountain

An Amish Man of Ice Mountain

The Amish Heart of Ice Mountain

An Amish Courtship on Ice Mountain

An Amish Match on Ice Mountain

And read more by Kelly Long in

An Amish Christmas Quilt

The Amish Christmas Sleigh

The Amish Christmas Candle

The Amish Christmas Kitchen

An *Amish Wedding Feast*

ON
ICE MOUNTAIN

KELLY LONG

ZEBRA BOOKS
KENSINGTON PUBLISHING CORP.
www.kensingtonbooks.com

ZEBRA BOOKS are published by

Kensington Publishing Corp.
119 West 40th Street
New York, NY 10018

All Kensington titles, imprints, and distributed lines are available at special quantity discounts for bulk purchases for sales promotion, premiums, fund-raising, educational, or institutional use.

Special book excerpts or customized printings can also be created to fit specific needs. For details, write or phone the office of the Kensington Sales Manager: Attn.: Sales Department. Kensington Publishing Corp., 119 West 40th Street, New York, NY 10018. Phone: 1-800-221-2647.

Zebra and the Z logo Reg. U.S. Pat. & TM Off.
BOUQUET Reg. U.S. Pat. & TM Off.

First Printing: December 2019
ISBN-13: 978-1-4201-4129-0
ISBN-10: 1-4201-4129-5

ISBN-13: 978-1-4201-4130-6 (eBook)
ISBN-10: 1-4201-4130-9 (eBook)

10 9 8 7 6 5 4 3 2 1

Printed in the United States of America

Prologue

Holmes County, Ohio

The air in the sick room was suffused with the pungent smell of mixed herbs and camphor. Ransom King lifted his *grossdauddi* into a more comfortable position on the bed, then watched as the old man smiled and focused his bleary blue eyes. "So, Ransom, tonight I think we finish this battle and I *geh* to rest from my labors."

"Don't talk like that."

"But you know it's true, my *buwe*." The *auld* man coughed and took a few moments to regain his breath. "So, let's speak of something else then, eh?" His grandfather stroked his long white beard and looked up into Ransom's face. "The women of our community all think you hate them."

"That's what you want to talk about?" Ransom sat down carefully on the edge of the bed and stretched out his legs. "Women?"

"*Jah*, women—they are important, my *buwe*."

"Fine."

"Ach—" His grandfather waved a dismissive hand. "What is this 'fine'? It's been nearly five years, Ransom.

Long enough to let *geh* of the things that haunt you and to go home to Ice Mountain."

"Some things become part of your soul."

Ransom looked away, taken back five years to memories he usually tried to avoid. When he finally realized his grandfather had made no answer, he glanced down to find that the man who meant more to him than any other had slipped peacefully away . . .

Chapter One

Ice Mountain, Pennsylvania

The hot sunshine of the summer Thursday morning caught on the glassware and flower petals that gave special significance to the corner of the King kitchen where the *eck* table stood.

All that was needed was the bridal couple and their attendants to begin the special wedding feast at which Jeb and Lucy King would receive the blessings and well wishes of both family and community.

But the wedding ceremony still went on, as it normally did, for a *gut* four hours, and Ransom King was bored. Despite having only just returned to Ice Mountain after a five-year stay in Ohio, he found that Amish weddings seemed pretty much the same in both places. He let his gaze roam over the profile of the groom, his handsome big *bruder,* and then paid brief attention to the sound of Bishop Umble's exhortation. Idly, he glanced across the row at his fellow attendant, whom he was to escort for the day—Beth Mast.

The girl's plump cheeks were flushed a becoming pink and her small hands were clenched in her lap as she sat, as attuned as a baby hare to every moment of the long service. The last time he'd seen her, she'd been about thirteen and always seemed to be laughing, but there was something now about her tense face that made him think she didn't laugh much anymore.

Then, something seemed to come over the girl. Her face drained of color and she wobbled slightly in her hard-backed chair.

She fell, like a wilting rosebud, slightly sideways, soon destined for the floor but for Ransom's quick reflexes. He caught her neatly, ignoring the surprised whispers behind him, and pressed the back of his hand to her forehead as he lowered her gently to the wooden floor. Then he slid two fingers past her *kapp* string and felt for the pulse in her soft neck; he found it strong and steady. "Fainted only," he pronounced quietly, thinking that Bishop Umble would probably continue with the ceremony whether one girl fainted or ten.

"She needs to eat," Ransom commanded softly over his shoulder to an elderly woman, aware that the girl had most likely been too focused on her duties as attendant to eat any breakfast. It took a few moments, but then someone passed forward a small glass of water and a morsel in a white cloth napkin. *Gut,* he thought. Water first. He coaxed it between her lips and her eyelids fluttered. Then he checked in the napkin. Great. *Pie.* He pressed some crumbs to her lips and she opened her wide blue eyes in both dawning surprise and dismay.

"Blueberry pie . . . ach, my . . ."

Ransom stared down at the intriguing freckles on her pert nose. "Oh my, indeed."

"I have to get up," she whispered in visible desperation, obviously taking in the fact that a leaning circle of onlookers had their eyes on her.

"Fine, get up, but you're coming outside with me for a breath of fresh air," he muttered. "I'll wager the *gut* bishop has about forty-five minutes left in him yet." He started to lift her and could tell she was about to protest. He bent his mouth to the delicate ear nearest him. "We don't want to make more of a scene, do we?"

Her gentle face flushed with new color as he drew her upright, catching her hand against the crook of his arm and escorting her down the open aisle between the massed chairs with confident aplomb. It didn't matter to Ransom that there were titters of interest as they passed; he was used to giving the older hens something to talk about. But as soon as he had Beth safely outside in the gentle breeze, he realized that the girl had no desire to make a spectacle of herself.

She drew her hand from his arm and swiped at her eyes. "I've ruined my best friend's wedding."

From another girl, the statement might have been considered dramatic, but Beth's soft voice was subdued with sorrow that somehow struck a resonating chord in Ransom's usually immune heart. He clenched his jaw and reached a hand to rub back and forth across her back until he felt her spine stiffen.

She looked up at him with something akin to shock. "You're touching me."

He gave her a sour smile. "I also touched you when I helped you up from the floor. Remember?"

"Ach . . ." She covered her face with her small hands in obvious frustration, then mumbled, "You don't have to be so nasty."

He blinked. "Ah, so the little hare has teeth. Interesting . . ." He removed his hand from her back. "Would you like some water before we *geh* back inside?"

"*Jah.* Please."

He stalked to the well and removed the cover, then brought up the bucket and got her a dipperful. "Here." He offered it to her without preamble.

He watched as she lowered her hands, took the dipper, then drank thirstily; she put the back of her hand to her lips when she'd finished.

After a moment of silence, she spoke up softly. "I should tell you that I'm sorry about your grandfather dying; it must have been difficult."

Ransom shrugged. "He was old, sick, and in pain. It was a blessing."

"I see . . ."

He had to smile; her tone was haughty. "Not much on the niceties, am I? But I do remember that your own *daed* was killed the summer I went away to apprentice with my grandfather. I'm sorry, Beth."

He noticed that she had suddenly gone very pale, but she nodded just the same. "Thank you. I—I'd like to *geh* back in now."

"Of course." He offered his arm. "By all means, let's *geh* back."

"*Danki*," she whispered, reaching a hesitant hand to his sleeve.

As her fingers settled on his arm, he decided with a strange certainty that Beth Mast was more than blueberry pie crumbs on pale lips and a soft back beneath light blue fabric—she hid something. But whatever it was, it mattered little to him, and he marched her purposely forward. . . .

Beth stared down at the steaming plate of ham, mashed potatoes and gravy, corn, green beans, and cucumber relish that her stepmother, Viola, slid in front of her as she sat at the *eck*. Beth was surprised at the sudden kindness of her stepmother but then winced at the older woman's words.

"You've got to eat, Beth—after that terrible fainting spectacle. My, people will think I don't feed you enough." Viola gave a soft laugh and drifted off into the crowd. Beth watched her go with a churning in her belly. She had no desire to let anyone see her gobbling up food. Nee, *I'll take a plate home for later and eat it in my room.* The thought made her feel less anxious as she watched Viola move about the crowd.

Viola had been her stepmother since Beth was five. Beth's own *mamm* had died of influenza before that, and her *daed* always said that he had been blessed to meet Viola and her seven-year-old daughter, Rose. Beth knew her *daed* was right—that Viola was a blessing—especially since her *daed* passed away five years ago . . . She felt tears sting the backs of her eyes at the thought of her father's

accidental death. Nee, nee *accident;* nee *accident* . . .
She toyed with her fork, pressing its metal handle
deep into her palm to remind herself that she was
alive . . . Of course, her father had left them all
well provided for, but Viola and Rose were frail.
And Beth was glad to be needed as she helped with
the running of the family's home and caring for
their few farm animals, even though she grew tired
sometimes.

She jumped a moment later, though, when Lucy,
the bride, leaned close to her.

"What did Ransom say to you outside, Beth?"

Her best friend's voice was a conspiratorial
whisper, and Beth forced herself to smile. "You're
supposed to be thinking about your wedding day—
and being Lucy King now."

Lucy shrugged her delicate shoulders, and Beth
watched her best friend's eyes sparkle with love for
her new husband. "I know, but I would also like to
see you perhaps become part of the King family.
Ransom is a catch—even if he is, well . . . closed to
people since he's *kumme* back."

Beth couldn't contain the blush she knew heated
her cheeks, but she answered easily. "Which is exactly
why he would never have eyes for me. . . . He was just
being kind."

"Well, he's going to have to be 'kind' all of today.
You know he's to be your escort for everything—
oops, and here he comes now to sit by you." Beth
tensed up with stress when Lucy withdrew and as-
sumed a proper bridal expression.

"Are you feeling better?" Ransom asked quietly
as he maneuvered his long legs over the bench
and under the table. He set a loaded plate in front

of himself and gave her what appeared to be an intent look.

She swallowed. "I—I'm fine. *Danki.*"

"Are you?" he asked. "Because you look like you're about to throw up. Are you nervous with me, Beth?"

She felt a flare of anger inside but resolutely pushed it down. She shook her head primly. "I'm not in the least . . . nervous with you. And thank you for being so kind as to help me this morning."

He shook his head. "Back to being the quiet little hare, are you? Why have you changed so much since you were thirteen? I remember you as a laughing girl with a sparkle in those big blue eyes. What happened since then?"

What happened to me? What happened to me? She felt her hands begin to shake and moved to clench them nervously in her lap. She struggled to speak for a moment, but then swallowed down the emotion. "It's a wonder you remember me . . . It seemed you were always stuck on my *stepschweschder.*"

"Who? Rose? Rose was—and I bet she still is— a brat."

"How dare you insult Rose?" Beth felt herself almost get to her feet. She hadn't really wanted to be Lucy's attendant—there was too much stress—but she'd done it because she loved Lucy. Now she wanted only to flee the crowd and the conversation and the infuriating man in front of her.

"Going to run away?" he asked in smooth tones.

She blinked, wondering how he could read her so well.

"I'm going to sit here and eat and do my duty as an attendant at my best friend's wedding. That's all. . . ." *And I'm going to ignore you! You with your dark good looks and firm hands and* . . . She broke off her thoughts, appalled at herself.

But he nodded. "Yes, it feels as though I'm losing my own best friend. Jeb and I were always pretty close . . . And I know why you didn't eat. Like as not, you were doing what I was doing—couldn't even have a forkful of scrambled eggs because I was so busy helping Jeb get ready."

Beth heard the warmth in his voice when he mentioned his older *bruder*. She knew there were two years between the older King *buwes*—Jeb at twenty-six and Ransom at twenty-four.

"You—you must love him very much," she said. *There, that's the polite thing to say* . . .

Ransom smiled, a casual lift of his lips that produced an indentation in his cheek that made Beth think of an errant little boy.

"Ach, I do—of course. And I'll miss him, though he'll only be down the way at Lucy's place."

"Will he work at the woodshop as well as farming?" she asked, unclenching her hands a bit.

Ransom shrugged. "Probably. Especially if he needs more money when the *kinner* start to come."

Beth felt her face flame. Rarely had she known a man to be so matter-of-fact about the appearance of children. She wasn't sure how to respond.

"Put a foot wrong, didn't I?" Ransom laughed low. "I apologize."

"*N–nee,*" she protested feebly. "It's fine."

"You'd think at your age it would be more than fine. You don't believe babies come from beneath the cabbage leaves, do you?"

Her anger at him was back and she set her lips in a thin line. "Of course not," she muttered.

He laughed. "*Gut!*"

She sighed, wishing she could be witty and charming somehow. *At my age . . . why, I could slap his face . . . even though everyone in the community probably thinks I'll die an* auld *maid. . . . Die . . . It should have been me . . .*

Then she noticed that Ransom had raised his small punch glass in one of his big hands. "Then here's to knowing where *kinner* come from, eh?"

She looked in his handsome face and saw the twist of his lips as he gave the toast, and she saw something like a dark flame in his eyes, but just as suddenly, it was gone.

She grabbed her glass, sloshing the liquid a bit over her hand, but then determinedly clinked her glass against his and put the strawberry punch to her lips. She'd never had anyone offer a toast in her direction and the feeling was heady.

"To *kinner*," she returned, watching his tan throat work as he swallowed. And suddenly, she realized that she'd hurt him somehow with her "hare's teeth" and the toast, but she couldn't understand why. And she had little time to ponder the feeling as the wedding festivities continued.

Wedding days were a time for games and fun, and some girls of the community, despite his position as escort to Beth, tried everything they could to catch Ransom's interest. He was brushed against, forced to catch someone with a sprained ankle, had his suspenders snapped against his chest, and one female actually whispered something in his ear that did not bear repeating.

"I feel like I'm being mauled," he muttered softly to Beth, who stood quietly by during all these ploys. "Let's *geh* for a walk."

Beth nodded, and he was surprisingly refreshed by her silence. They wandered along the grass near the green trees, and Ransom found that he couldn't think of much to say until she asked him about his apprenticeship.

"Ach, now that was something both hard and worthwhile. I plan to expand Daed's woodshop to include the making of fine furniture, mantelpieces and scrollwork for larger houses. My grandfather was a *gut* teacher. . . ."

She nodded. "It must have been hard, though, to be away all those years and then to nurse your grandfather. I—forgive me. That's just something I heard, and—"

"Of course I nursed the *auld* man," he said easily. "I loved him and he had no one else." Ransom cleared his throat. "And what of you, Beth Mast? What are your plans in life? Surely not to stay under Viola's thumb forever?"

She sucked in a deep breath and was about to make a sharp retort when she felt him lift her chin with one of his hands. "I mean no disrespect. . . . It's a genuine question."

"I—I expect that I'll always be with Viola. She needs me, needs what I do around the *haus*." *And I'm scared, afraid to think about being alone. I don't want to be alone.*

She parted her lips and drew in her breath as she came back to the moment. Ransom leaned closer to her, then released her chin. She was unsure what game he was playing at, but his attention made her feel out of control and she didn't like that one bit. She took a step backward and promptly tripped over a large, exposed tree root. She felt herself falling, but Ransom grabbed her arms and pulled her back to her feet with inexorable strength.

"You need to drink more water," he commented.

"I tripped—on this root! I didn't faint and don't think for one minute that I was trying to get your infernal attention," she huffed, moving away from him.

"We'd better *geh* back to the wedding, unless you'd rather stay and . . . talk?"

She gritted her teeth and shook her head, not understanding why the man so infuriated her. But soon they were back among the crowd and she could concentrate on her role in the wedding party.

It was late when the wedding celebration was over, but Beth had done her duty as attendant and visited and laughed shyly with everyone she knew. Lucy had also led her inside to see some of the wedding gifts, which would ultimately have to be moved to the newlyweds' cabin. The bride and groom had definitely been blessed with gifts to start a new life.

"Beth . . . Allow Rose to lean on you as we walk. She's tired and you're so much more—hearty." Her stepmother's voice cut through Beth's wandering thoughts.

Beth swallowed and nodded as Viola turned away.

It was time to say goodbye to Ransom and she wasn't quite sure of how to do it properly.

But he took sudden charge of the situation by catching one of her hands in his and then giving her a faintly mocking bow. "Goodbye, Beth. Have a *gut nacht*."

"Ach, *jah*," she murmured, flustered. "*Gut nacht*."

Chapter Two

As dusk set in and the fireflies began to dance, Ransom eased the curry brush down the side of his faithful horse, Benny, and let his thoughts drift back over the day's wedding. Beth Mast had proved a dutiful companion for all the games and visiting that went on, and he wondered at himself for baiting her. He was still considering this when his seventeen-year-old *bruder*, Abel, came in with a bucket of oats and hurriedly fed Benny.

"You going down the mountain to Coudersport tonight, Abel?"

His brother stopped in his tracks and Ransom frowned. Abel was having his *rumspringa*, and Ransom knew only too well that the unaccustomed freedom of this time could lead to reckless behavior.

"Uh . . . *jah.*"

"To meet a girl?"

Abel nodded. "Mebbe."

"Do you have protection?"

"Uh . . . I . . ."

Ransom blew out a breath in exasperation and gave his *bruder* a pointed look. "Condoms, Abel?" He took out his wallet and withdrew a few bills. "Get some. And don't forget to use them . . . It's easy in the—moment to let seemingly lesser things *geh* by the wayside."

"All right. *Danki*, Ransom."

Ransom sighed to himself once Abel had gone and then dropped the curry brush and pressed his head against Benny's side. The vast emptiness he always felt and could never seem to push away rose up in his throat and he choked on a half sob. Some days, he didn't know how he was supposed to go on. Once more he wished that the ground might cover his back and hide his face forever. . . .

"You all right, *sohn?*"

Ransom looked up and quickly put on a mask of composure as his father came into the barn and set a lantern down on a barrel top.

"*Jah*, Daed. I was thinking more than working, truth to tell."

"Well, it'll be strange not to have Jeb in the *haus*, that's for sure."

"Uh—right."

"Not what you were thinking of?" His *fater*'s voice was warm. "Perhaps it was the bevy of young *maedels* there today? Or one in particular?"

"*Nee.*" Ransom laughed. "No one special."

"So I won't be gaining another *dochder*-in-law anytime soon?"

Ransom put down the brush and went over to lay a gentle arm round his *daed*'s shoulders. The *aulder* man had recovered from a heart attack recently and sometimes seemed more fragile than Ransom cared to acknowledge.

"No, Daed. If there's ever any girl I come to love,

I promise you'll be the first—or somewhere in the top three—who *kummes* to know it."

They laughed together and then headed for the *haus* in the gloaming. Once there, Ransom sat down to the table to enjoy a cold supper of stewed tomatoes and sugar, egg salad, hearty bacon and broccoli salad, and a blueberry cake for afters. The blueberry cake made him think of the moment he'd fed Beth the pie after she'd fainted. *Little hare . . . somewhere along the way she's lost her spark for living . . . like me . . . I know it. . . .*

His *mamm* was quiet, obviously tired after a day's helping at the wedding, and Ransom gently patted her shoulder as he got up to take his dishes to the sink. He bent and kissed her soft cheek, balancing his plate in his left hand. "*Danki*, Mamm—for all of your hard work. I know Jeb and Lucy appreciated it."

"As well they should," his sister Esther mumbled sourly, her irritability bearing witness to her own tiredness.

Ransom laughed. "*Kumme* on, Esther. You know you loved every minute of it."

"Better watch out, Ransom King," Esther quipped, "or you're going to get trapped into a wedding of your own one of these days."

She got up from the table and swatted at him with a damp dish towel. He easily evaded her, then jumped up to sit on the wooden counter, swinging his legs. "You be older than I, Esther . . . Isn't it time you yourself were, uh, trapped, as you put it?"

His sister glared at him. Everyone knew Esther was moody and scared off any prospective suitors with her sharp tongue, but Ransom still thought she was beautiful—even if a bit off-putting. But now, she marched from the kitchen, obviously dismissing him in a fit of anger.

"Ransom, you shouldn't tease her so," his *mamm* said in soft rebuke as she pumped water into the sink.

"I know." He grinned. "But it's too much fun to stop."

"Well, while you're having fun, I need you to remember that I want you to take some lamb's ears plantings over to Viola Mast's *haus* tomorrow. She asked for them special today, and you also need to return the tables we borrowed."

Ransom jumped down from the counter and headed for the stairs with a yawn. "No problem, Mamm. *Gut nacht.*"

He expected to drop right off to sleep, praying that he would find solace in oblivion. But it was like always—he'd awaken after an hour or two, then pace the floor until he lay down in utter exhaustion while still finding no comfort in his bed.

Beth finally fell asleep after tossing and turning for a *gut* hour while images of the wedding day and Ransom King were dancing shadows behind her eyes. But then, as usual, the nightmare began, and she was trapped between the mattress and the quilts with nowhere to run in the confines of her mind.

She could smell the blood—a tangy, metallic scent that made her long to curl up in a ball. But she couldn't . . . She waited for the familiar jolt and the scream of the horse, and then she was free and running, always running far, far away. . . .

* * *

Dawn had yet to stretch its pink fingers across the summer morning sky when Beth slipped quietly from her bed. She was grateful for the feel of Thumbelina, her large Maine coon cat, when he brushed against her legs in the inky darkness. She dressed with hasty hands, anxious to get the milking done before breakfast. Friday meant doing the laundry—always a prodigious task, but today, with the addition of the soiled tablecloths Viola had loaned and brought back from the Kings', it would be a monstrous chore.

But Beth was undaunted; she understood that work was a necessary thing in life. And, as her *stepmamm* often said, "The more time spent in work, the less there is for idle thought." Beth had no desire for idle thoughts. She liked to keep her mind busy and in control. She knew that if she let her mind wander, she wouldn't like the dark trails it would roam, so she was happy for the often heavy chores.

Thumbelina jumped ahead of her as she carefully made her way down the ladder from her loft bed-room in the big cabin. She gained the main floor, avoiding the particular floorboards that creaked in an effort not to wake her *stepmamm* and Rose. The two had large bedrooms, and, as was typical, they each had placed a mound of clothes and linens out-side their respective doors the *nacht* before so Beth might gather their laundry without waking them before breakfast was ready.

She balanced the tall pile of clothes and walked blindly toward a small door. The washroom was adjacent to the kitchen—a cramped space, barely big enough to hold the wringer washer, large tub, and, when needed, the ironing board and heavy irons heated on the woodstove. She had to go outside, through a narrow back door, to pump the water, but she understood Viola not wanting her to use the kitchen pump and possibly slosh water on the hickory flooring.

Beth dumped the clothes down and hurriedly tiptoed back into the main kitchen. There was part of a pumpkin pie left from yesterday, and her mouth watered in expectation. She stood at the clean counter and, after saying a quick grace, wolfed down the thick, soft filling. She felt the familiar satisfaction of temporary fullness, then returned hurriedly to the laundry.

It took five pails of water to get the metal tub full enough for washing, and she hastily separated the whites from the colors after lugging the buckets to the tub. She plunged the first of Rose's dark aprons into the water, watching the fabric balloon up, then squashing it down once more. She continued through dresses of different hues, then paused for a moment to catch the breeze from the open back door. Just then, Thumbelina let out a piercing meow.

Beth jumped in spite of herself, then stepped outside in time to see Ransom King driving a wagon slowly down the dirt lane that led to the barn. The clip-clopping of the horse's hooves was muted in the morning's newness. Ransom gave her a casual wave and she lifted her hand, feeling a strange pounding in her chest. She was suddenly very conscious of the perspiration stains under her arms and the fact that her hair had escaped her *kapp* in errant tendrils.

"He must be returning the tables from the wedding to the barn," she muttered to Thumbelina, who purred loudly in return. "And he probably won't even stop here at the cabin . . ."

Still, she grasped her hair with ruthless fingers and hastily pinned it back as best she could, then returned with a resolute effort to the washing. She was working the wringer washer when a male voice sounded from the doorway, and Thumbelina's purring increased.

"That's a big cat."

Beth spun, then swallowed hard, careless of the water dripping from the pillowcase she held.

"Uh . . . *jah.* . . . His name is Thumbelina. I–I thought he was a girl at first and then . . ." She floundered helplessly, wishing she could be as beautiful and confident as her stepsister.

Ransom smiled and stooped down to rub his hand in the thick gray fur of the animal, and Beth was reminded of his stroking her back on the previous day.

"I came to put the tables in the barn, all right?" He slanted a glance up at her through thick lashes, and she wet her lips.

"*Jah*, do you need any help?"

He rose and shook his head. "*Nee*—it's men's work anyway."

"Ach, I'm as strong as an ox," Beth returned in a cheery tone, unconsciously repeating what Viola had often said.

She watched him as he let his dark eyes skim down her damp frame and up again. He shook his head. "I don't know who's been putting such ideas in your head, but whoever they are—they're wrong. You look like you should be cutting flowers, not doing such heavy labor as this." He gestured to the wash piles, visible inside the door. "Where's your stepsister to help?"

Beth drank in the kindness of his words and then snapped back to the moment. "Ach, Rose is delicate—a doctor told her long ago that she should only do light tasks as she tends to faint . . . And by the way, she is not a brat."

Ransom gave her a wry look. "Uh-huh," he said, then reached out to gently tug the wet pillowcase from her fingers. "What do you say to the two of us getting this job done faster?"

Beth stared at him, appalled. "I couldn't— couldn't let you help me."

He put his hands on his lean hips, ignoring the dripping cloth he held. "Don't be ridiculous. I did my grandfather's laundry for years. . . . *Kumme*, let me show you."

"But—it's women's work."

He laughed then. "I guess, in truth, that work is work. But I can do this more easily than you—not to mention faster. So why shouldn't I help?"

Then she watched helplessly as his light blue shirt became wetter and wetter as he took charge of the wringer and soon had the clothes flying through.

"This is not what I expected of the man who baited me yesterday," she finally blurted out.

He paused and looked down into her eyes. "Do you want me to stop?"

She could have kicked herself, but she answered anyway. "*Nee.*"

"*Gut,*" he said and resumed working. "Can you hang these on the clothesline?" he asked over his shoulder, and she hurried to help.

She swallowed when she saw that he held one of her plain *nacht* shifts in his big hands. He gave her a wicked smile and lifted it to her as she flushed. She grabbed it without a word and was stretching to place a wooden clothespin when she heard Rose's voice and spun in dismay, thinking desperately of a way to explain why Ransom King was washing women's dresses and undergarments.

Chapter Three

Beth wanted to dissolve into a spot on the clean grass, but instead she swallowed and walked over to the small washroom. Rose stood like some kind of fairy apparition in the doorway, the early sunlight playing off her magnificent red hair, which hung unbound down to her hips. She was wearing her dressing gown but was standing with visible confidence as Ransom paused, looking unimpressed, with a dripping cloth in his hands.

"What's going on this fine morning, Beth?" Rose's voice was high and breathy, and Beth ignored the fact that any other girl would have run back to her room if caught in such a state, with her hair loose, as only a husband should see it. But not her Rose . . . *Nee*, Rose had both confidence and innocence, Beth thought with pride.

"Ach . . . Ransom offered to help with the washing and I . . ."

"Let him, of course." Rose smiled. "What kindness, so early in the morning. You must *kumme* in and have some breakfast, Ransom. I'm sure all of this work has made you hungry."

Beth watched Ransom wring out the towel he held

and then look up at her stepsister. *Heaven only knows what he's thinking . . . Surely he must be floored by Rose's beauty despite thinking she's a brat. . . .*

"Breakfast would be nice," Ransom said. "You go on and cook while Beth and I finish here."

Beth hastened to intervene, feeling flustered. "Ach, but I do the cooking. I'm sorry, Rose—I forgot breakfast with this pile of laundry, and—"

Rose waved a delicate hand in dismissal. "I'll cook, Beth. Please *kumme* in, Ransom, and dry off. Beth's *gut* at the washing—she's used to it. Besides, I wanted to talk to you about making a new spice box for the kitchen—a surprise for my *mamm*'s birthday."

Beth grabbed the towel from Ransom's hand. "*Jah,* please *geh.* I'm fine here."

She felt him give her a measuring glance; then, finally, he nodded. "All right. If you're sure."

She watched them enter the *haus* in single file through the narrow door, and then Rose gently closed it with an innocent look, leaving Beth standing, feeling appropriately shut out of any such intimacies as morning conversation and flowing hair. She turned with a resolute face back to the washer and tried to ignore Thumbelina's plaintive meow.

"Well," she said, finally looking at the cat. "That was that."

Ransom knew he had a reputation since his return to Ice Mountain—that of being an available bachelor—but the overt manner in which Rose Mast paraded about the kitchen in her dressing gown made him long to run back outside. He wondered rather uneasily where Frau Mast was as Rose reached over his damp shoulder to gain the salt shaker for the scrambled eggs she was making.

"I can cook, Rose, if you'd like to—get dressed," he said finally.

But Rose appeared oblivious to her immodest hair and attire and waved airily at him. "Ach, I'm quite comfortable, Ransom. But you must be feeling damp in that shirt. Why don't you—"

Ransom was spared any suggestion on the girl's part when Viola Mast entered the room from the staircase, apparently without noticing him seated at the table.

"Rose, whatever are you doing? You know it's Beth's job to cook. Where is that laz—" With a start, she caught sight of him. "I mean . . . girl?"

Ransom watched Viola change facial expressions as fast as a shadow slips out of the sunlight. And he felt troubled. There was something going on in this *haus* of women that made him worry for Beth. *Not that it's any of my business . . .*

Viola continued. "Why, Ransom King—I didn't see you there. Rose, dear, run along and dress and I'll check whether Beth needs any help and take over here."

"Ach, Mamm, I'm fine. Don't be so stuffy. Ransom's seen a woman's hair before, I'm sure."

He didn't respond to the loaded comment but rubbed absently at his wet sleeve.

Viola took the moment into her own hands with a none-too-subtle pinch to Rose's arm. "I must insist, Rose. Now, *sei se gut.*"

Rose flounced to the door of her room with a smiling backward glance in his direction; then he rose from the table bench. "I'll *geh* help Beth finish the washing while you cook, Viola."

He didn't know how Viola might have responded because Beth emerged from the washroom just then.

"Ach, there you are, child," Viola practically cooed. "*Kumme* sit down with our guest and have something to eat. You must have been up quite early."

Ransom didn't miss the surprise on Beth's face and then the flush of happiness. "*Danki*, Viola. . . . *Danki* for getting breakfast, and I'd love to sit down, but I'd better *geh* and change."

Ransom cleared his throat. "You wouldn't be the only wet one at the table."

She looked at him with her wide blue eyes, and he was reminded of a baby owl peeking out from its nest.

"The eggs are ready now, child. I'm sorry, Ransom— forgive my negligence. Beth must indeed change, as is only proper."

He sighed to himself, then pulled his pocket watch out. "Well, now that I look at the time, I'd best be getting back to the woodshop. I left the lamb's ears plantings you wanted in a box on the front porch. I'd love breakfast another time. *Danki*, ladies." He turned and made for the front door, but not before he'd taken a last long look at Beth.

"You simply must finish up the breakfast, Beth— I'm having those pesky chest pains again," Viola said. "You may change later. I'll *geh* and sit in Rose's room and you may serve us there."

Beth murmured a reply, still thinking about the fact that Ransom King had helped her do the wash, when Viola paused, then raised her voice slightly. "Ach, and Beth . . . perhaps you don't understand what's proper with young men—you've had so little experience. . . . But a *maedel* does not let a man help her with such menial chores as the laundry. It is not fitting."

Beth bit her lip, thinking of Rose in her dressing gown, then nodded. "*Jah*, Viola. It won't happen again."

"*Gut*. I'm glad to hear it." Viola disappeared into her room, and Beth bowed her head. It was a shame that it would never happen again—she'd rather enjoyed working side by side with Ransom King, even if he seemed difficult to understand at times. Then she hurried to salvage the burning toast.

Twenty minutes later, she hefted a loaded tray of crisp bacon, scrambled eggs, grilled tomatoes, toast, and homemade marmalade and managed a soft knock on Rose's door.

Rose bade her enter, and Beth got the door open, balancing the tray on her hip. Neither Viola nor Rose looked up when she got the tray into the room and started to set it up on the small wooden table by the window, reserved for such occasions.

Rose popped off the bed, now suitably dressed, with her hair *kapped*, and snatched a piece of bacon from a plate. Beth watched her in some dismay, knowing that no grace had been given for the food. But Viola seemed willing to overlook the infraction as she calmly took a place at the table.

"That will be all, Beth. *Danki*."

Beth nodded, preparing to leave the room, when her stepmother's voice gave her pause. "Ach, and Beth, I know you planned on attending the blueberry frolic tomorrow, but I'm afraid that I must *geh* to chaperone, of course, and that black-faced sheep of yours is about due to drop her lamb. Someone should watch her."

Beth felt her heart sink. The blueberry frolic was one of the social highlights of the summer, but she couldn't deny that Cleo had been showing signs of being near to giving birth and she might need help.

"Viola, perhaps Jimmy Stolfus could stay with her." Jimmy was the twelve-year-old *buwe* who'd been hired to help Beth about the farm.

She watched Viola smile. "Now, dear, you couldn't possibly know that I gave Jimmy the day off tomorrow, and besides, Rose will bring you back some berries for jam. Won't you, Rose?"

"Mmm-hmmm," Rose mumbled, her pretty mouth full.

Beth nodded her thanks and left the room, closing the door quietly behind her. It's of no matter, she told herself stoutly. *I probably wouldn't have had too gut a time anyway.* But then, Ransom King's smiling face danced before her eyes, and she had to push the thought away with deliberation before heading back downstairs to clean the kitchen. Once there, she took a brief moment to snatch up the last of the crisp bacon and sank to the floor, her back to the cupboard as she ate the salty meat. Thumbelina came purring and she split the last bit with the cat, then slowly got to her feet once more.

Chapter Four

Saturday morning dawned bright and clear. Ransom worked the hook and eye closures on his dark green shirt and thought about the annual youth berrying frolic that was planned for the day down in Stout's Hollow. Picking the ripe berries was a fun chore, made even lighter by the laughter and good-natured teasing that usually echoed through the trees. Of course, he was long past youthful activities, but he had it in mind to *geh* along, chaperone the *buwes*, and get some fishing done.

Ransom's mind slipped back to the last berrying he'd been to on Ice Mountain. He'd been sixteen, nearly seventeen, and preparing to leave home to apprentice at his grandfather's woodworking shop. He remembered, with sudden clarity, that Beth had not been among the gaggle of girls who attended the frolic. Then he admitted to himself that he'd enjoyed baiting her at the wedding, just to see the life spark in her eyes.

He slid his suspenders up and headed out of his room. His *mamm* met him in the kitchen.

"You can't *geh*," she said.

"What? Where?"

"To the berrying. I'm sorry, Ransom, but I just got word that your Great-Aenti Ruth is being trundled up the mountain this morning from over Coudersport way. She couldn't make it to the wedding because of a migraine, so she's coming now."

Ransom longed to groan aloud. "Aenti Ruth? Mamm, she's all of about a hundred and is meaner than a cold snake on a hot Sunday. Can't Esther stay here with her?"

His *mamm* turned and started to pile things into a wicker picnic basket. "Esther can't deal with Aenti Ruth as well as you can, and you know she gives your *fater* stress—which he should not have after his heart attack. Besides, he got a rush order at the woodshop this morning for some cabinetry from a *gut Englisch* customer."

"Then I should help him, not stay in here and babysit the family pit viper."

"Ransom!"

"All right, I'm sorry."

"Look, *kumme* late to the berrying. Aenti Ruth usually takes a long nap in the afternoon. Get her settled and—and that'll be that."

"*Jah.*" He sighed. "Mamm, do you remember the last time Great-Aenti Ruth visited? You have to admit she's a bit, well—odd."

"Eccentric," his *mamm* corrected and swatted his arm with a roll of tinfoil. "And when you get *auld*— you'll be . . . odd too. Now I have to get a move on. I promised to help chaperone the berrying with Viola Mast."

"*Jah* . . . and I told Abel I'd chaperone the *buwes.*"

"Well, I'll keep an extra eye out," his mother promised.

Ransom saw his day's plans melt away, but he couldn't very well leave his *mamm* in the lurch. His great-*aenti* was a handful, but he'd always been able to roll with her . . . oddness and somehow escape the lashing of her sharp tongue.

He exhaled and took a poppy seed roll from the plate on the table after his *mamm* and Esther had gone. Then he wandered outside to the woodshop while he waited for the impending storm that was Great-Aenti Ruth.

Ransom walked into the woodshop and saw his *daed* working on a piece of cherrywood, carefully sliding a lathe down its edge.

"Ach, so it's Aenti Ruth coming, *sohn*?"

"Ya, Daed, I heard . . . your favorite relative." Ransom smiled.

His *fater*'s brown eyes twinkled as he turned the wood. "You know, Aenti Ruth seemed *auld* even when I was a *buwe*. As a matter of fact, I recall getting the idea that she might be *auld* enough to enjoy a *gut* joke." His *fater* smiled in remembrance.

"What happened?"

"Typical boyish prank. I caught the biggest bull-frog I could find down at the pond, lugged him home in a bucket and put him in Aenti Ruth's bed— down where her feet would touch. I waited for the scream I knew was coming—but none came. Then I got nervous. As the *nacht* wore on, I couldn't sleep because I was so nervous. My mind went in all sorts of directions 'til I thought maybe that frog had killed Aenti Ruth somehow and I'd be responsible. I finally fell asleep, and then it was morning and Mamm called breakfast. I stretched, and then my feet hit something cold and slimy and I nearly raised the roof with my scream. Here, Aenti Ruth made friends with that frog and put him right back with me—odd bedfellows we were that morning!"

"Did you get in trouble?" Ransom asked, laughing at the story.

"*Jah*—had to make beds for a month. And Aenti Ruth left me all kinds of surprises in the quilts."

"Surprises?"

"A bat, a giant spider, and ten salamanders, to name a few. I tell you, that woman isn't *gut* for a body's peace of mind."

Ransom was still chuckling when a wagon drew to a stop outside the shop. The driver set the brake with a wrenching sound, and Ransom nodded to his *fater*. "You keep working, Daed, and I'll *geh* and greet her."

"I think I'll take you up on that. *Danki, sohn.*"

Ransom went outside and reached for his wallet for money to pay the driver, but the man waved him off with a fast hand.

"Shhh," the man hissed. "She's fallen asleep in the back on the hay—either that or she's dead . . ." the *Englisch* man muttered in hopeful tones.

"Okay, well, why don't we—" Ransom choked on his words as dogs began howling and a pink pig leaped from the side of the wagon, hitting him square in the chest with a *gut* hundred pounds, squealing like there was no tomorrow.

Ransom staggered back and tried to arch his neck away from the animal, which seemed bent on kissing his face.

"Now you've done it!" the driver hollered, adding to the sudden fray.

Ransom tried to put the pig down, but it clung to him like a limpet. Then he looked up as Great-Aenti Ruth stood up in the back of the wagon. Ransom could see that she held the leashes of three assorted hounds in one hand and a large guinea pig in a bird-cage in another. Her wrinkled face was cracked in a smile, and Ransom watched as a green parrot flew off her shoulder to *kumme* and land on his head.

"Well, well," Aenti Ruth screeched. "Ransom King. You've grown up some and Petunia likes you—that's something."

"You mean your parrot?" Ransom gasped as the pig began snorting and pawing in an effort to dislodge the bird.

"*Nee, buwe*, that's Jack. Petunia's my pig. Now carry her in the *haus*."

Ransom couldn't figure anything else to do but obey and walked slowly away, but not before he caught a distinct gleam of pleasure in Aenti Ruth's bright, hawkish blue eyes.

Beth pushed down a new wave of disappointment as Rose airily waved goodbye from the buggy Viola was driving. Perhaps it was fitting that she stay home. . . . *Perhaps* Gott *has something different in store for me today* . . . It was a thought she often used to comfort herself, and it helped as she looked for opportunities to do a kindness or speak a word of cheer to others. It was hard, though, to put Ransom King and his dimpled smile out of her mind, so she headed off the porch for the smaller barn, intent on checking the pregnant sheep, Cleo.

Beth slipped off her normal shoes outside the barn and stepped into the too-large mucking boots that always stood ready for her small feet. She entered the barn quietly, leaving the door ajar, not wanting to disturb the sheep, especially Cleo, who had a tendency to bolt at the slightest odd noise—especially when she was expecting.

Beth grabbed a handful of sweet hay and approached Cleo's pen. The black-faced sheep stared up at her balefully, her stomach visibly distended. Beth clucked with sympathy and unhooked the pen, only to jump in alarm when a strange squawking echoed through the barn. A green parrot flew in and landed with apparent purpose on Beth's shoulder, causing Cleo to take off at top speed.

"What? Ach, *nee*. . . . Cleo!"

Beth tried to shoo the strange bird away, but it clung resolutely, its small claws clutching at her *kapp* strings. It held on as she staggered out of the barn in her big boots, intent on catching Cleo, who tended to have difficult deliveries. But the sheep was determined to bound through the field, despite her pregnancy. Her wooly hind legs kicked up clods of mud and growing plants with splattering abandon.

"Cleo!" Beth called, finding herself losing ground. But she kept on, and eventually reached the edge of what she knew to be the Kings' property. The faint and awful thought of possibly meeting Ransom in her mud-soaked dress was quickly dismissed as the small parrot let *geh* and flew off in the direction of the Kings' big log cabin. Beth stopped to catch her breath, and Cleo chose that moment to begin circling the mud in a strange dance that Beth knew was natural for the sheep just before birthing.

Beth closed her eyes briefly, muttering a small prayer that all would *geh* well with the sheep, then sank to her knees to await what she hoped would be a straightforward delivery.

Chapter Five

"Ach, there's Old Jack now on the screen door," Aenti Ruth commented from where she'd ensconced herself in the kitchen. "Fetch him in, Ransom."

Ransom stifled the urge to send the parrot packing; he'd been delighted when the bird dislodged itself from his shoulder a *gut* half hour ago. And judging from the warbles, whistles, and shrieks the creature made through the screen door, Ransom could only suppose that Jack had spent the last thirty minutes gathering the local gossip from the resident birds of the area. When he opened the door, expecting the parrot to *kumme* back inside, Old Jack did no such thing, but instead shrilled all the more fiercely and flew off toward the fields.

"Don't just stand there, *buwe*," Ransom heard Aenti Ruth snort. "Fetch him back, I say."

"*Jah*," Ransom muttered, feeling that his world had turned upside down and his feet were in the sky. He headed out at a jog, seeing the parrot as a distant green speck, dipping and circling amid the fresh green of the field. "Stupid bird," Ransom muttered, knowing he was too *auld* for such a chase. But then Old Jack seemed to lose speed and gently flew toward the ground ahead. Ransom was about to give vent to more emotion when he heard the distinct baaing of a sheep.

He slowed his gait and broke through the thigh-high corn only to stop and stare at the strange scene before him. Beth Mast knelt on the muddy ground while Old Jack perched casually on her shoulder. A lambing ewe added her noise to the parrot's squawks and Ransom raised his eyebrows.

"Beth? What *en der weldt* is going on?"

She turned to look up at him and her fair skin flushed pink, but she answered all the same. "This is Cleo—she's having a rough delivery as usual. I think it's twins, and the legs are in quite a tangle. I don't know about the parrot. . . ." She made an ineffectual attempt to tip the bird off her shoulder and Ransom frowned, snapping his fingers.

"Jack! Here!" He realized he sounded like he was calling a dog, but to his surprise, the parrot responded and left Beth to perch on Ransom's shoulder.

"Ach . . ." Beth muttered, clearly focused on Cleo. "He's yours."

"*Nee*, but he'll not bother you now." Ransom dropped to his knees in the mud beside her, and Beth shook her head in distress.

"Ach, you needn't get all dirty. I can manage, I think."

"All right, have you had a go yet?" he asked, and she nodded.

"I can't quite sort out the legs."

"Do you mind if I try?" Ransom swept his gaze over her. She was dressed in an odd shade of pumpkin and still managed to look pretty, even with a splotch of mud on her cheek. He cleared his throat and saw that she nearly jumped.

"*Nee* . . . I mean, *jah*. Go ahead, but she may kick. Cleo gets particular when lambing doesn't go right."

He nodded as Jack gave a conspiratorial squawk, clearly in favor of a kicking Cleo. But now Ransom focused on the ewe, ignoring the parrot on his shoulder as he tried to help the lambing process move in the right direction.

Beth clasped her hands in her muddy lap as she watched Ransom gentle Cleo with soft, soothing sounds from the back of his throat. Then he was carefully undoing the muddle of the baby lambs.

"*Jah*, twins," he murmured. "And all I've got to do is figure out which legs are which."

Beth waited and pulled long leaves from the cornstalks to create a makeshift bed for the lambs as he brought them into proper position and then moved aside to let nature have its way. Cleo delivered the twins in quick succession and then lay down on her side in preparation for nursing.

"It usually takes a *gut* half hour for a lamb to nurse," Ransom said, and Beth nodded, watching him wipe his hands in the mud. She did the same after a moment, knowing the rich earth had more healthy bacteria in it than one could imagine and was a good substitute when water wasn't available.

"Where did you get the parrot?" Beth asked, breaking the silence as she caught him studying her with some sort of speculation in his dark eyes.

Ransom smiled, and she thought how impossibly

handsome he was as she struggled to hold his gaze. "It's a long story, but the more important question is, why aren't you at the blueberry frolic?"

She did look down then, twining her muddy fingers together. "Viola thought that Cleo might lamb, and she was right. I'm glad I was here," she said simply. Then she looked up. "Wh–why aren't you there yourself?"

"Family business, now finished, I hope. Anyway . . . why don't you *geh* home and wash up and change? I'll do the same and then we'll go to the frolic. It's not too late."

"But what about Cleo?" Beth protested, though her heart was beating fast. *Stop being foolish*, she admonished herself. He's only offering you a ride and not suggesting that you *geh* together—together. . . . Still, her mind whispered, no one—no man—has ever suggested any such thing before. . . .

Ransom waved a hand toward the ewe and her lambs. "I'll head back to the house, take the parrot with me, and return with the wagon. I'll pick up Cleo and the twins and bring them over to your barn, safe and sound. What do you say?"

Beth found his questioning smile contagious. "All right." She mentally thumbed through her chores for the day, then reassured herself that Viola would surely be glad she had been able to go berrying after all. She started to struggle in the mud to get to her feet when she found herself lifted from the ground as though she weighed nothing more than thistledown. She stared up at Ransom and watched in fascination as he swiped a long finger across the mud on her cheek, then wiped his hand down the front of his green shirt.

"Well, Beth Mast, we make quite a pair, wouldn't you say?"

She nodded, then smiled with the heady feeling that bubbles were popping in her throat. "*Jah* . . . a pair."

Chapter Six

Ransom bathed hurriedly and pulled on a light blue shirt. He'd already taken the wagon and settled Cleo and the lambs in the Mast barn, and now he hoped that Aenti Ruth would be napping in the family room.

He tiptoed past Aenti Ruth, asleep in his *daed*'s favorite chair. The posse of hounds lay in various comedic poses at the *auld* woman's feet. Old Jack was drowsing atop the birdcage, and Petunia snored and sighed. *All I have to do is get past her without making a single*—"Wheek! Wheek!"

Ransom nearly jumped out of his skin. He'd forgotten the miserable guinea pig! And now the entire rabble was chorusing together. Aenti Ruth opened her blue eyes and fixed him with a grim look. "Going out, young man?"

Ransom came forward, bent to pet the smallest hound, and nearly lost a finger in the process. "Foul beast!"

"Not so," Aenti Ruth said easily. "No one likes to be shaken from their sleep, but now that we're all up—where are you off to?"

"Uh—just to the berrying frolic—probably a lot of bugs . . ."

"*Gut*," Aenti Ruth declared. "The dogs like to bite the occasional bee in half—poor creatures. We'll *kumme.*"

Ransom closed his eyes briefly against the image of Aenti Ruth and company joining the blueberry frolic. *And what will Beth Mast say?* He pushed this last thought aside without stopping to think why, and then set about cajoling Aenti Ruth into changing her mind.

In the end, a triumphant chorus of animals and bird alike heralded his passage on the road to get Beth, and he felt a headache begin to pulse behind his eyes.

"Why you were ever stuck on that redheaded Mast twit is beyond me." Aenti Ruth's comment intruded on his head pain, but he had to smile.

"Rose? I was a kid and, as I told Beth recently, the girl is a brat."

"Beth cannot say boo to her own shadow," Aenti Ruth grumbled, and Ransom turned to look at her sideways while he held the reins with ease. "At least that was the way she was the last time I visited."

"Oh, I don't know," he said easily. "Sometimes it's the smallest creatures who have the most dangerous bite."

"A ha!" Aenti Ruth grinned. "You like her."

"Like her! Liiike her!" Jack mocked, and Ransom wondered how best to kill a parrot without leaving any evidence.

"Of course I like her. She was the other attendant at Jeb and Lucy's wedding."

"Which gave you proper time to develop an interest," Aenti Ruth said with smug assurance.

Ransom decided that the best course of action was to remain silent. He knew that Aenti Ruth meant no harm and probably had no way of knowing about his past. . . .

Beth bit her lip in brief indecision as she glanced at the meager selection of dresses in the chest at the foot of her bed. She finally drew a breath and reached below some of the carefully mended pieces to lift up a sweet blue garment. She'd never worn it before and, in truth, had forgotten about it until now. She'd stitched the dress from a bolt of fabric that Rose said she didn't want because it did not *geh* well with her hair, and Viola hadn't wanted it either. So, it had been given to Beth. She hoped her stepmother would be pleased that she had done something useful with the fabric.

Beth hurried to change and then glanced in the small mirror above her dresser. She saw that even her white prayer *kapp* had not escaped Cleo's lambing and was splattered with mud. Beth took another from the top drawer of her dresser and hastily redid a few hairpins before fitting the *kapp* into place. "There," she said aloud, and Thumbelina meowed his approval. Beth smiled and headed back down the loft ladder to the kitchen.

Viola and Rose had asked her to pack a picnic lunch for them for the blueberry frolic, and now she realized she needed a basket of her own. *And maybe Ransom will share* . . . She giggled aloud at the absurd thought, then realized there was no harm in pretending she was preparing a lunch for the two of them. She had very keen ideas about what should *geh* into a picnic dinner, though Viola and Rose preferred the traditional fried chicken and cold salads. Beth, on the other hand, decided on fresh bread and pimento cheese, purple grapes from the arbor, little paper-wrapped cones of almonds, and a bottle of fresh lemonade. She hastily added linen napkins to the other cutlery, then snapped the lid closed on the basket. The sound of hoofbeats on the dirt road could be heard passing the window and Beth grabbed the basket, bid Thumbelina goodbye, and hurried outside, anxious not to keep Ransom waiting.

Beth had seen a circus once as a young child, and as she stood on the bottom step of the porch, she thought she was seeing one again. She stared in fascination at the moving image of the Kings' wagon, with Ransom and his Aenti Ruth riding on the high seat with a large pink pig sitting between them. Ransom looked grim, but Aenti Ruth seemed to be having a *gut* time with the now-familiar green parrot on her shoulder. A strange combination of sounds came from the vehicle, and Beth was trying to sort out the noises when the wagon ground to a halt as Ransom set the brake hard.

Beth watched him jump down from the high seat and walk toward her. Somehow, she felt as if his dark eyes drank in her person, and she knew she flushed, as was becoming a habit when near him.

"Your dress is beautiful." He said the words softly to her, and Beth nodded her thanks, unsure of how to respond to such praise. She had always been taught to guard against vanity. Then Ransom gave her a stiff bow and extended his hand. "Milady of the blueberry blue dress . . . your carriage awaits."

Ransom was torn between irritation and an odd sense of fun as he led Beth to the wagon of mayhem, but he gave in to the humor as he felt Beth's hand in his and stopped a few steps from handing her up.

"Beth Mast, *sei se gut* allow me to introduce my— extended family. Great-Aenti Ruth, I believe you know from past visits. That shoulder-perching pal of a parrot is Old Jack. And Petunia the pink pig will not gladly surrender her seat to you, but she does like to give snout kisses. The three hounds hanging from the back are Matthew, Mark, and Luke—Matthew bites. The tailless fur ball in the birdcage is Pig—just Pig, don't ask me why. Have I missed anyone, Aenti Ruth? Hmmm?"

Ransom laughed in the face of the daggers that flew at him from the keen old blue eyes.

"I believe, Ransom King, that you may accompany Petunia in the back of the wagon and Beth shall drive." Aenti Ruth's tone dared him to contradict.

"Liiiike her! Like her!" Old Jack mocked, and Ransom frowned, wishing he might toss Aenti Ruth and the parrot into the back with the hay, but instead he smiled good-naturedly.

"All right, Beth . . . Can you manage Benny and the reins?"

Beth nodded, looking confused, and he concentrated on handing her up into the wagon. Then he swung into the back and unceremoniously grabbed Petunia and hauled the protesting pig into his lap.

"Ladies," he called over the barking, squealing, wheeking, and squawking. "Let's *geh* to the blueberry frolic—I'm sure it will be one that none of us shall ever forget!"

Chapter Seven

Beth focused on the reins between her fingers, feeling rather nervous of Aenti Ruth's closeness. The last time she had met the *auld* lady had been about two years before, when there'd been a community picnic. Aenti Ruth had demanded fresh lemonade, fresher than what was being served, and Beth had gone to make it with pleasure.

Now, Beth nearly jumped on the wagon seat as Aenti Ruth laid a bony hand on her knee and leaned close to speak above the noise of the animals.

"You've become more beautiful, child, since I saw you last."

Beth smiled uncomfortably. *Beautiful? What is it to feel beautiful and not hollow inside? Not to feel separate and naked?*

Aenti Ruth gave her knee a sharp tap. "Feeling beautiful comes from an inner knowledge, Beth Mast, though I doubt you've ever been given a chance to cultivate such thoughts." She sighed and withdrew her hand. "Still, you're a *gut* girl, and there's something to be said for that."

"*Danki*," Beth murmured, feeling confused and

wanting to change the subject. She felt as if Aenti Ruth's words were stones thrown at unbreakable glass, and she refused to drink them in. "Your—animals are unique."

"Ach . . . not animals—family. Family! I nearly lost my mind when my dog John had to be put to rest. He had an enlarged heart, but he was a faithful *buwe* to the end."

Beth smiled. "I love my cat, Thumbelina, the same way. He's a Maine coon."

"Beautiful," Aenti Ruth said, nodding her bonneted head.

"Here we are," Ransom called, breaking into their conversation over the skirmishing sounds in the air.

Beth pulled gently on the reins and crossed the short wooden bridge that led to Stout's Hollow on the east side of Ice Mountain. The cool, shady place, so right for blueberries to grow, soon enveloped them in the heady scents of summer.

Beth eased Benny into a shady spot, and she noticed that Ransom was out of the wagon in an instant, taking the reins from her and tying them on to a low-hanging branch. She watched as he swung Aenti Ruth to the ground and then turned to look up at her.

"And now our fair driver." He reached strong arms up and caught her waist, and, before she could protest that she was too heavy, he'd lifted her down with a warm smile.

Beth swallowed, touched by his expression. But then she bit her lip. Maybe Viola was more than right in saying she had no experience with men, for certainly Ransom was simply being kind—as he would be to any girl. And, as if to prove her unspoken thought correct, two girls Beth knew from church meetings came up to the wagon, smiling at Ransom, twisting their *kapp* strings and talking in a manner that was alien to Beth.

"Ach, Ransom, will you *kumme* and share our picnic *sei se gut?*" one girl pleaded, reaching to touch his sleeve.

"Well, I'd normally love to, girls, but I must settle my *aenti* and see my mother for a moment."

Beth thought his dark eyes danced with merriment, so that he really did look as though he was promising the girls something.

"*Jah*, Ransom," the other girl cooed. "We surely have the sweetest place to sit—right by the creek."

Beth looked at the ground, then snapped up her head when Aenti Ruth cleared her throat. "Leave with what little humility you possess, you twits. Ransom is engaged in unloading my animals."

"Liiike her. Liike her!" Old Jack crowed, then flew to sit on Beth's shoulder.

The girls frowned, but then walked off giggling, and Beth heard Aenti Ruth tsk at their lack of modesty. "Ransom, if you spend your time with the likes of those creatures, you surely will *geh* down a peg in my estimation."

Beth said nothing but noticed that Ransom didn't speak either. *Well, why should he deny it? He's handsome—they're pretty. Like likes like, after all. . . .* She resolutely lifted her chin, then wondered if she was simply being too self-involved. Old Jack seemed to feel her mood shift because he sidled down her shoulder and plucked at one of her *kapp* strings.

She laughed out loud and felt her good humor renewed.

Ransom frowned as he began to hoist the animals out of the back of the wagon. He grew tired of the virtual attacks of the women in the community. At least Beth was demure, though he knew she had a temper as well. He half-shook his head, berating himself for even thinking about Beth. *She doesn't matter. No girl will ever matter again. . . .*

Yet he couldn't help but admire the gentle downward stroke of her lashes as she accepted her picnic basket from him, and he had a vague idea that he might like to see what she looked like after having been thoroughly kissed.

"Liiike her!" Old Jack squawked, but Ransom ignored the bird and put a hand on Aenti Ruth's elbow, only to have it immediately brushed aside. "I'm not some two-toed sloth that has to be led across the field, *buwe*! I *geh* at my own pace."

"*Jah*," he muttered and glanced at Beth, only to see a faint smile playing at the corners of her pink lips. It made him smile too, and he handed off the hounds' leashes to his *aenti* and leaned close to Beth.

"Do you too *geh* at your own pace?" he asked softly. "Or may I take your arm?"

"I—"

"Ransom!" Aenti Ruth crowed. "There's your mother coming, and you know she's only going to fuss. Head her off with Petunia, who'll probably eat from everyone's plate anyway!"

Ransom reluctantly obeyed, moving from Beth's

side to put Petunia on the ground. The pig immediately took off, leaving faint screams and scuffles in her wake. Ransom watched his *mamm* stand, obviously torn between the pig and the advancing human pit viper, and realized he'd now have a chance to talk to Beth alone. But when he turned, he found her gone. He scanned the groups of picnickers and Amish women with blueberry baskets on their arms and finally located Beth with her stepmother. *It looks like Beth is being lectured . . . naturally. . . .*

He edged closer and ran full tilt into a feminine body. He looked down at the red-haired girl in his arms and stifled a groan. *Rose Mast . . . and she looks like a cat ready to have Old Jack for dinner. . . .*

"Really, Beth . . . I cannot think what came over you—arriving at the frolic in a wagon, with Ransom King and that *aenti* of his . . . and that dress . . ." Viola picked sharply at Beth's sleeve. "Why, this blue is hardly your color, my dear."

Beth felt her eyes fill with tears. She'd been so sure Viola would be glad she'd done something worthwhile with the castoff fabric. "Perhaps you're right, Viola," she murmured. "I—I suppose I could have used the fabric for quilt squares or something. . . ." Beth ruthlessly squashed the memory of Ransom telling her the dress was beautiful and felt like running home.

"Well, you're here now . . ." Viola spoke in measured tones. "You might as well *geh* and pick enough berries for jam. You won't have time for that lunch basket, so hand it to me, *sei se gut.* I can hardly think what got into your head . . ."

Beth gave Viola her lunch basket in exchange for an empty picking basket. She drew a deep breath and nodded in agreement with her stepmother. "*Jah,* Viola—I'll *geh* and start picking the berries."

She bent her head and walked away toward the laden bushes, choosing to move a distance from the happy young people gathered. She was wishing vaguely for Lucy's company when she heard Rose's light laughter. Beth saw her stepsister standing near Ransom. She couldn't see his face, but he appeared to be listening intently to everything Rose was saying, and Beth turned away, unsure as to why she felt such frustration at the sight.

But she shook off the thought and concentrated on picking berries. There was a certain knack to picking blueberries—they hung on the bushes in bunches like grapes, and Beth knew the secret for getting the ripest ones. She held her basket in one hand under the berries and with her other hand, she cupped a bunch and gently rubbed them with her fingers. The ripe berries dropped into her basket while the unripe ones remained attached to the bush.

She had picked about half a gallon when she heard the genial call that it was time for picnic lunches, and she moved farther from the others, following the trail of ripe berries. She told herself that she was definitely not feeling as hungry as her rumbling stomach suggested and tried not to think about her picnic basket. She was resigned to doing her work as her stepmother bade her. She entered a small clearing near the creek that bubbled lazily through the hollow and saw some ripe blueberries hanging just out of reach. She stepped carefully out onto a semiflat, wet rock and reached for the fruit . . .

Chapter Eight

Ransom blinked at the verbal assault both Rose and her mother were conducting. Clearly, they wanted the pleasure of his company and were willing to say anything to get him and the suddenly present Petunia to take a seat on their picnic blanket. But Ransom was adept at dealing with women, and he put those skills to use now.

"Ransom." Viola gestured with an elegant sweep of her hand. "We have plenty of space, and your dear mother and I have much to attend to in chaperoning this boisterous group. Why not *kumme* sit with Rose while I check with your *mamm* about how things are going?"

Ransom raised an eyebrow and watched while Rose smoothed down the skirt of her green dress. She'd arranged herself in a pleasing pose on the edge of the blanket, right next to what he recognized as Beth's picnic basket.

"I'm sorry," he began in smooth tones. "I'm sure my mother is occupied at the moment with my Aenti Ruth, but I wonder if I might do you both a service and fetch Beth back for the picnic—so we can all enjoy the day together?"

Rose burst out. "*Nee*, but you can *kumme* and sit—"

"Rose, dear," Viola interrupted hurriedly. "Of course the picnic would not be complete without sweet Beth. We do appreciate your efforts, Ransom."

"Great. *Danki* to you both." He rounded the blanket with casual steps. "I'll take her basket—in case she's wandered far and wants a snack." He lifted the basket with two fingers and gave them both a wide smile.

Viola nodded. "*Jah*, by all means, take her basket. The child tends to get overly hungry—her size, you know . . ."

Ransom stifled the urge to dropkick the basket at Viola's head, told himself that no *gut* Amish man would ever think such things, and was off with a simple wave over his shoulder. He quickly left the other youths behind and wove in and out of the bushes and ground cover. He hiked for a *gut* quarter mile, far from the crowd and Viola's prying eyes.

He was surprised when Bishop Umble came whistling toward him out of the woods. The *auld* spiritual leader had a handful of blueberries and paused in his whistling to chew.

"Ach, Ransom! How are you?"

"Fine, sir."

"Yet you're far from the gathering—though perhaps there's other fruit you'd rather pick, hmmm, *buwe*?"

Ransom felt cornered somehow. Bishop Umble's bright blue eyes gleamed with strange secrets, and for a brief moment, Ransom wanted to back away.

The *aulder* man laughed softly. "You're gun-shy, Ransom, and I wonder why—though I suppose everyone fears something from their past. . . . Well, happy picking!"

Ransom eased a breath from his throat. He recalled now that even as a young child, Ransom had felt that Bishop Umble was . . . odd in his perceptions.

Then a suddenly present Petunia snorted from up ahead and gave a faint squeal as Ransom heard a subdued female cry and the distinct splash of water.

He broke away from his thoughts and hurried through the blueberry and laurel bushes. When he came to the edge of the water, he saw Beth teetering on a slippery rock with one foot in the water and one out.

He dropped the picnic basket on dry ground and caught her by the waist, preventing her from getting completely wet. She shook out her blue dress and mumbled a shamefaced "*Danki.*"

"You always seem to catch me at a falling-down moment," she muttered.

He laughed gently, turning her against his body, then risked lifting her chin so that her wide blue eyes stared up at him with visible confusion. "I prefer to think I catch you falling up."

"What do you mean?"

He looked at her thoughtfully. "I seem to have the privilege of helping you when you're doing something to lift up the world—like being a friend's wedding attendant, or helping Cleo, or picking blueberries out here alone while everyone else is eating."

She nodded, blushing. "*Danki*, but you should be eating too."

"As should you," he said roughly and regretted his

tone when she brushed past him to reach for more berries.

"My stepmother—Viola—she wanted me to get enough berries picked for jam, and because I came late, I—"

"I have your picnic lunch," he interrupted, swinging the wicker basket up from the ground.

"Ach, you shouldn't have, Ransom. Viola asked me for it and . . ."

"She gave it to me quite willingly and we—are going to eat, right now. Besides, it will give the hem of your dress time to dry in the sunlight. And—I'll help you pick berries to make up for the time you spend eating with me."

She was still hesitating when Petunia came grubbing back through the low blueberry bushes. "See, we have the pi—Petunia to chaperone. I promise I'm not as bad as my reputation suggests. *Kumme*, I'll *geh* and find us a spot to enjoy our picnic."

Beth sat down carefully on the gray rock Ransom indicated as he passed her the picnic basket. She had, in truth, never shared such intimacy with a man—even when Ransom had helped with the washing, she'd been aware of her family in the *haus*. Yet she also felt comfortable with Ransom—a feeling she could not quite explain. Though he was mocking at times, he was also truly a gentleman, which helped her confidence a great deal. She found that he filled in the gaps of conversation and covered for her shyness, slowly drawing her out like a budding rose to the summer sunshine. . . . *I feel different with him . . . but it can't last. . . .*

"So, Beth, what do you like to do with your days?" he asked as she passed him a linen napkin.

She shrugged. "I suppose what any Amish woman does—housekeeping, farm chores, and ach . . . baking." She said the last with fondness and caught Ransom's dimple as he smiled.

"Baking was something I did for my grandfather. I actually enjoyed it a great deal," he explained.

They were both silent for a moment then, giving thanks for the food.

"What do you mean?" Beth asked after she lifted her head. "You enjoyed it? Surely it's a woman's chore and must have seemed tedious to you."

He waved a hand at her and gave a low laugh. "Ever practical, little hare, aren't you? Why should it have been tedious when it played on my senses so very well? Touching . . . tasting . . ." He cleared his throat abruptly.

She wondered at his sudden halt, but then went on with the thread of the conversation. "There are the *gut* smells . . ."

"True," he muttered.

She watched his eyes darken as she spoke. "And hearing the oven heating or the timer ringing."

Ransom nodded but seemed suddenly tense, and she stopped speaking and bit her bottom lip.

"Did I say something out of turn?" she asked.

He shook his head, but she still felt his distance for some reason.

"My, but you're moody at times," she said plainly.

"What?" His voice was low.

"Nothing. I shouldn't have said that."

"*Nee.*" She watched him arch a dark eyebrow at her. "Say whatever you please."

"Look, should I just *geh* back to picking berries?" Beth asked, lifting her chin.

He was silent for a long moment as he looked at her. "No, please don't go. I am moody. You can hurl all the abuse you want at me and half of it would probably be true."

"Ach, I doubt that. I spoke out of turn."

"All right, let's call truce and *geh* back to baking . . . What's your favorite thing to bake?"

He felt on safer ground when she smiled widely. His own talk had heated his awareness of her and he shifted uncomfortably on the rock when she spoke.

"Ach, that's easy . . . pie."

"My favorite too." He laughed, telling the truth. "Mark Twain said that 'Pie needs no advertisement' and he's quite right."

"What pie do you like best?"

He smiled and reached beside him to pull a handful of ripe blueberries down from a bush. He opened his hand and held it out to her. She chose two berries with her slender fingers and popped them into her mouth. He did the same and felt himself shiver suddenly. *If I were a superstitious man, I'd say I just made some sort of heart pact with Beth Mast over a handful of blueberries. But that's just wishful thinking . . . I can never . . . never . . .*

"I love blueberry the best too," Beth confided, breaking into his thoughts. She poured some still-cool lemonade for him as she spoke, then looked him square in the eye. "Lattice crust or whole?"

"Lattice," he pronounced solemnly.

"You're so right!"

She seemed about to continue when Matthew came bounding into the clearing. He began to bay nosily, and Ransom tossed him a crust of bread, which Petunia scrambled to steal.

"Ach, Ransom—I'd better *geh* back. Viola will certainly be looking for me. *Sei se gut* enjoy the rest of the lunch."

He watched her get to her feet, then set off with quick steps to the trail between the bushes. She called an echoing *gutbye*, and Matthew howled in accompaniment.

Ransom looked down at the lemonade in his cup, then shook his head at the two animals. "If she knew me for what I truly am, she'd never sit with me like this," he muttered aloud, and Petunia grunted in placid agreement.

Chapter Nine

Beth sought the solace of Cleo's small barn in the twilight of the evening. She had two buttered corn muffins in a napkin and ate them quickly, sharing the crumbs with Cleo. She drew in a deep breath and felt better as she rubbed her stomach.

Against her will, the memory of her father at the reins of a buggy flashed behind her eyes, and she swallowed hard, pushing the image deep inside her mind, wishing she had brought another muffin to the barn.

Then she carefully petted the now-soft heads of the cleaned twins and listened to the ewe's gentle baaing. The noise soothed her rattled nerves after the lecture Viola had given her following the blueberry frolic. Beth shuddered as she remembered her stepmother's chiding words with stark clarity.

"I don't know what everyone must have thought, Beth! Delaying Ransom from coming back to our blanket was both inconsiderate and tiresome."

Beth had nodded, making no excuse. She realized she probably *had* delayed Ransom by almost falling into the creek and knew that she had lost track of time in his company.

"*Jah*, Viola," she'd murmured.

"Ransom King is kind and a gentleman, of course. He no doubt thought you needed to have something to eat before you returned. You must try to control your appetite, Beth—both for things of the world and more food. Do you understand?"

Beth had murmured "*Jah*" and was glad she'd been bidden to *geh* see to the sheep without having dinner, though she'd managed to sneak the corn muffins from the hutch.

Now she let Cleo nudge her away from her babies and Beth wondered again what Viola had meant about "things of the world." She hadn't dared to ask, but perhaps Lucy would know. She'd be glad to see her newly married friend at Sunday church meeting the following day. She left the small barn and crept back into the *haus*. She longed to cook something on the stove but knew the smell would drift to Viola, so she heavily sugared a heaping bowl of blueberries and climbed to her room to hurriedly eat the snack.

She knew that gluttony was a sin and surely she was guilty of the act; she forced herself to slow down as she ate the food. She felt a sudden wave of distaste for herself but finished the berries. She ran a finger around the purplish sugar granules at the bottom of the pale blue bowl and thought about Ransom's dark eyes. What would he think if he knew how much she ate in secret? She shuddered to herself at the idea but sucked the sugar off her fingertip just the same.

Ransom played with a loose harness while watching his older *bruder*, Jeb, bed down the horses. Ransom had dropped off the rest of the family, animals and fowl included, and had walked the mile to Jeb's new *haus*.

"So, how's married life?" he asked without preamble as he walked into the big barn.

His *bruder* raised a dark brow at him in the mellow light of the kerosene lantern. "That's what you came to talk about?"

Ransom shrugged. "Why not? I've never been married . . ." He broke off and caught up a curry brush to groom the nearest horse.

"Ransom, I know you couldn't *kumme* home because Grossdauddi became so ill, but what happened to you there?"

Ransom felt a chill creep down his spine. "What do you mean?"

"You're different. I don't know exactly how or why, but there's something . . . dark in you. I've been meaning to talk with you, but the wedding came first and—"

"I grew up," Ransom said softly, terrified that Jeb would start asking more questions.

Jeb shook his head. "Hey, when you want to talk about it, you know I'm always here."

"I'm not trying to put you off," Ransom lied with the ease of long practice.

"I believe you—I want to believe you."

"I'll say *gut nacht*, then, big *bruder*." He dropped the brush on top of a nearby barrel. "Give my well wishes to your wife."

"*Gut nacht*, Ransom."

Ransom went out into the dark. He took a long time to walk home, even as he struggled to contain the tears that stung at the back of his eyes. *I'm fine* . . .

fine . . . fine. The refrain echoed in his brain and matched the cadence of his lonely steps.

Beth paused with a foot on the last rung of her loft's ladder, trying to get the empty bowl from the blueberries back to the kitchen. She swallowed a surprised gasp as Rose's door was flung open. "Beth, where have you been? I've been waiting for you to brush out my hair. And why did you have that bowl up there? Didn't you eat enough at the frolic?"

Beth tried not to hear her stepsister's question and set the bowl on Rose's dresser. She bent with automatic fingers to pick up the array of dresses that had been left on the floor. Rose was not the neatest person in the world, Beth considered, but she more than made up for it with her beauty and poise.

"Ach, leave those dresses, Beth. I'm tired after today, and I had to scrub for nearly ten minutes to get the berry stains off my fingers. It looks like you haven't even begun to wash. What have you been doing, for mercy's sake?"

For a surprising flash of a second, Beth almost blurted out an angry reply, but then she remembered that her Rose was guileless as a child, and because of her weak health, no doubt had little idea of the chores Beth had to do each *nacht.*

"Well, Rose, I tended to the sheep—Cleo had twins, you know . . . and I cleaned up the kitchen and set the oats on to get ready for breakfast, and I—"

"Beth! Don't tug so! And I wasn't asking for a detailed list of how you spend your time!"

"I'm sorry," Beth said with contrition.

"Huh! Anyway, Mamm says Ransom went to find you. Likely he has a penchant for strays . . ."

Beth gritted her small white teeth in sudden response as Rose rambled on. "He is so good-looking. I may plan to have him if I choose."

"If you choose?" Beth murmured. "Doesn't he have a choice?"

"Beth, I told you not to tug! And *nee*, he doesn't have a choice. I think I am beautiful enough to have any man I want, and why not the most handsome one in the community?"

"I–I don't know, maybe he—"

"Just braid my hair, Beth, and *nee*—you don't know anything about men, so hush!"

It was with sadness that Beth drew the hairbrush through the long red tresses and carefully created two thick braids when she had finished. Then, as Rose murmured under the quilt, Beth finished picking up the floor, blew out the lamp, and left the room as silently as she could.

She quickly snuck the bowl back to the kitchen for a quick wash and grabbed a teaberry cookie to take back up to her room. When she got there, she was happy to see Thumbelina curled up on her bed. She spoke softly to the cat before moving to open the window so the cool *nacht* air could enter. *Animals don't judge. They don't lift up your rock in the stream and peer at your underbelly, poking and prodding and teasing.* She closed her eyes as she ate the cookie in two bites, then hugged her arms around herself, but it made her feel uneasy to give herself affection, so she stopped.

She thought about what Ransom's Aenti Ruth had said about her animals being family and supposed the *auld* woman was lonely—as she herself grew lonely sometimes.

Then her thoughts turned to Ransom, and she went to her bed and whispered secret, nameless prayers into Thumbelina's ears and, more importantly, to the Heart of *Gott*.

Ransom prayed that *nacht* before he went to bed— he begged *Gott* to clear his mind of what his grandfather called hauntings. But he knew he didn't deserve to have his mind cleansed, so he turned his prayers to reach to others. He prayed for what he knew the Bible said about "deep calling to deep . . ." and the intuitive feeling he had that Beth somehow had lost her spark for living. But then he told himself that he was crazy and was simply doomed to walk the earth a broken thing until the end of his days . . . and, in that vein, he hoped his days were short. . . . *I don't deserve to live, yet maybe that is the punishment of* Gott—*to have to live . . .* Dark thoughts crept round his mind, thoughts he'd grown used to . . . *a gun, a jump, deep water . . .* But he was a coward and knew he would never have the guts to end his life—that act belonged to *Gott*. . . .

Chapter Ten

"How was the blueberry frolic?" Lucy asked the question with obvious eagerness as they stood outside the Loftus barn, where the church meeting was being held that week.

Beth was unsure how to respond. She wished for a quiet moment alone with Lucy, not being surrounded by the milling community waiting until it was time to *geh* inside. But, as usual, Lucy could read her face.

"Ach, Beth—you've got to tell me everything! It was so wonderfully strange not to be there because I'm not in the youth anymore . . ."

"*Jah*, you're an *auld* married woman," Beth teased.

"Did you see Ransom yesterday?" Lucy demanded in a hiss as people began to shuffle inside. Beth only had time to give her best friend a smile of acknowledgment before Lucy had to move off to sit with the married women, while Beth found a place on the backless bench with the unmarried ones.

It was odd not to have Lucy beside her, and Beth had a sudden and strange longing to be married herself. *I'd love to have a husband to kiss and babies to love . . . and why, exactly, are you thinking this way, my fine miss! Who will marry me as plump as I am? It's funny, but I don't remember worrying about my weight when I was younger—at least not until my* fater . . . She thrust the sudden, disturbing thought from her and instead tried to concentrate on the mental image of Ransom's dark eyes when he'd complimented her blue dress. The diversion worked all too well and she had to steal herself to listen to Bishop Umble, who was bringing the message. The bishop was a wise and kind man who brought thoughtful messages before the community as Derr Herr directed. Beth normally loved to listen to his genial, elderly voice, but today, she struggled to concentrate until she heard the text.

"Today, we hear from 1 Peter 3:3-4." Bishop Umble cleared his throat. "Your adornment must not be *merely* external—braiding the hair . . . or putting on dresses; but *let it be* the hidden person of the heart, with the imperishable quality of a gentle and quiet spirit, which is precious in the sight of *Gott.*"

Beth sat up straighter. It was rare that a message seemed to fit so closely with what she was struggling with in her own life—but here were the exact words that confronted her own self-doubt about her weight.

She watched Bishop Umble begin to pace back and forth before the community, as he normally did.

"Now, men, don't start to doze on me because you feel that this message is for the women gathered only. For surely, we all can seek to develop a quiet spirit. But let's consider Peter's *Gott*-inspired words. We are a community blessed with beauty—from the mountains to the green of the fields to the faces of our loved ones—all things that we can look upon. But who is this 'hidden person of the heart' in our own lives? Surely we all have hidden things about ourselves that we'd prefer others not to know."

Beth watched as the bishop's eyes swept over the people gathered and felt her heart begin to beat faster.

Bishop Umble continued. "But I believe that Peter is speaking here about who we are deep inside our hearts, in the place that only *Gott* sees. We do not, as humans, have the ability to see much past the outside of our friends, or our enemies, for that matter. Ach, but *Gott* sees the internal, the core, and He understands our motivations and desires, no matter how deeply hidden they may be. Derr Herr sees us at our least lovable but loves us anyway, despite our mistakes and failings. . . ."

Beth glanced up to see a thin beam of sunlight coming through a subtle crack in the barn rafters and felt a momentary revelation, as if Derr Herr spoke to her directly: *You have a gentle and quiet spirit, Beth Mast, and you are of great worth to* Gott. . . .

Ransom stood at the back of the barn with the other young, unmarried men. He could see Beth from behind, recognizing her from the back amid all the other *maedels*. The soft curves of her shoulders and the careful stillness of her posture made her stand out to him. He had the unholy thought of her waiting before him, clad only in a simple shift, but then he ruthlessly clamped down on his desire and exhaled in the coolness of the barn. The smell of hay filled the space, and a feeling of peace moved over Ransom in slow degrees, putting to rest, for the moment, the fitful unease that had bothered him in the preceding hours. Bishop Umble's even, sonorous phrases echoed within the sturdy barn enclosure and seemed to find foothold and purpose in Ransom's mind. He was surprised that the Scriptures should matter to him that day—usually he came to church meeting but felt as though he had no right to be there. He dreaded to think of *Gott* looking at him, so he normally kept his mind closed when the bishop spoke . . . but today—today he heard the Word of *Gott* on a different level, and it made him swallow hard with feeling. . . .

Chapter Eleven

The following morning, Viola announced that she and Rose were going to spend the day exchanging quilt squares on the far side of Ice Mountain with an ailing neighbor. "And, of course, Beth, you shall stay here and put up the blueberries. Mind that you make plenty of blueberry sauce and also pie filling. You're so much better at it than Rose or me. And we do both appreciate your serving our home in this manner."

"*Jah, danki,*" Beth murmured, feeling pleased that she would have a lot to focus on, and for a *gut* purpose. Indeed, she didn't mind working on the blueberries, but the kitchen would be lonely and it would have been nice to have someone to talk with. *Ach, well,* she thought stoutly. *I've got Thumbelina.*

She saw Viola and Rose off after she'd done the breakfast dishes, then went to the cool back porch to bring in the baskets and pails of blueberries that had been their share from the frolic—everyone picked, but then the bounty was divided among the community.

She gently washed and strained the berries, using careful hands to make sure that none of the fruit was bruised while she also removed any stems or leaves. Then, while the berries dried on the tea towels she had spread on the wide table, she got out the necessary ingredients for blueberry sauce. The sauce was a treat to have atop pancakes or fresh biscuits and was fairly easy to make.

She had assembled the sugar, vanilla, and cornstarch when she happened to glance out the screened kitchen window and heard the brisk sound of a man's whistling. She wondered if it was Ransom and felt her heart begin to pound. She quickly dried her hands and went out onto the front porch.

"Hello, Blueberry Princess," Ransom said lightly from where he stood at the bottom of the porch stairs. He was swinging a full bucket of blueberries back and forth, and Beth felt her cheeks redden with his casual banter.

"I've got some extra berries—Mamm and Esther have put up all that the pantry would hold, and besides, Aenti Ruth is driving them crazy in the kitchen."

"Ach, more berries . . . do you have any idea what I've got to do now as it is?" She bit her lip at the honest exclamation.

"Well, now—that's interesting. I bet the brat and your stepmother found something to do elsewhere rather than putting up the berries." He moved up two steps, and Beth swallowed as she briefly thought how long his legs were.

She dragged her gaze back up to meet his dark eyes and felt her blush increase. "Viola—they went to exchange quilt squares with Frau Stolfus. . . . The steam from canning always makes Rose feel like fainting."

"Uh-huh, well, I'm here and I'll be glad to give you a hand. Thumbelina can chaperone."

"Ach . . . I don't know—maybe we . . ."

Ransom had gained the top of the steps and now stood mere inches away from her. He bent to whisper softly in her ear. "You need help. You don't have to do everything alone."

"I don't mind the work," she claimed after a moment. "And without it . . . well, I would feel out of control, and that's not good."

Ransom straightened his back to stare down at her with his dark, dark eyes. "Why?" he asked. "Why is it bad to be out of control?" She had difficulty fathoming the incredible sensation when he brushed his mouth against her cheek and down the curve of her chin. "Why?" he whispered again, but then he seemed to snap back to attention, and she glanced up to see his frown.

"We'd best get at those berries," he muttered gruffly.

She nodded, completely flustered, and nearly stumbled as she made her way back to the kitchen door.

He caught her easily, one arm sliding around the gentle curve of her waist. He pulled her soft body against his chest and hips. He cursed silently, even as he lowered his head and breathed in the delicate scent of her hair at the base of her *kapp*; the scent of a woman . . . *It's been so long . . . so very long . . .* Awareness of the summer day faded to the back of his mind, only to be replaced with a burning need, but then reason took hold of his mind and he released her abruptly. The whole encounter had taken less than a few seconds, but it had rocked him to the core, and he tried to clear his throat when she caught hold of the doorjamb and turned to stare up at him.

"Beth, I'm sorry . . . for—well, the last few moments." He watched her give a quick nod of understanding.

"*Jah* . . . likely you were thinking of some other *maedel*." Her tone was matter-of-fact.

"Wait—what?" Her calm words penetrated his mind and he reached out to lightly grab her wrist. He couldn't resist running his thumb over her fluttering pulse point and half-shook his head as he felt his body ache with arousal for the third time in as many minutes. "I wasn't thinking of anyone else, little hare." *Only you . . . only you. . . .*

"Well," she said stiffly, as he released her wrist. "There are the berries to do, and I can do them alone, *danki*."

He nodded. "*Sei se gut*, let me help, Beth. . . . I promise I'll focus on the . . . work at hand. Please . . ."

"All right," she whispered, then widened the door and let him pass.

She let me in . . . she trusts me . . . like Barbara once did. . . .

He was suddenly transported in his mind to another kitchen, an *Englisch* kitchen—and Barbara urging him to get in as much kissing as possible before her father came home. He remembered the twinned pleasure of excitement and danger as he eagerly sought her mouth. . . .

Ransom came to himself in faint bewilderment—*I shouldn't be here alone with Beth . . . What am I doing?* He turned, intent on fleeing the bright and airy space, but then he saw Beth's face and the faint blush on the apples of her cheeks. He knew instinctively somehow that to leave her now would hurt her, and he didn't want that . . . no matter the cost to himself.

Beth followed his tall form into the cool kitchen and found, to her surprise, that her hands were shaking. She clasped them behind her back for a moment, then resolutely stepped to the table. Her normally work-driven mind was shaken by mental images of Ransom touching her and then. lastly, the abject fear of what would happen if Viola found out. . . .

Ransom clung to the present by concentrating on the particulars of the Mast kitchen. He noticed that everything in the tidy place was laid out neatly, as suited Beth, and he leaned against the table and asked what he might do to help.

"Well, I—" She hesitated, and he watched her thoughts play across her honest face.

"Are you making blueberry sauce first?" he asked in a gentle tone, and she nodded.

"Then I'll get the saucepan going and you throw in the ingredients?"

She nodded, clearly glad to be able to do something besides talking with him.

He discovered that he wanted to soothe Beth even as he himself found peace in her presence, despite the painful memories that had assaulted him.

He watched her small, slender hands add blueberries, water, sugar, and vanilla to the saucepan on the cookstove and for a dizzying moment saw her tending to heating baby bottles with the same competent care.

He dragged himself to attention when he heard her ask, for what must have been the second time, for the cornstarch. "Uh, sorry." He passed her the box. "Just thinking to myself."

She nodded. "So Aenti Ruth has her own recipes for things?"

"*Jah*." He smiled, glad for the turn in conversation. "And the recipe cards are in her dear *auld* head, so she shouts ingredients over the howling of the hounds—which she insists must be present—and my poor *mamm* can't take it."

"I like Aenti Ruth," Beth said with some asperity.

Ransom nodded. "I guess I do too—in a way." He watched Beth add another big handful of fresh berries and then helped her with the boiling jars. The heat flushed her cheeks becomingly and caused little wisps of hair to appear outside her *kapp*. He looked away from her, though, then helped to can the blueberry sauce with ease.

The morning flew past as jar after jar was filled. Finally, Beth spoke happily. "There! We've done them all. *Danki*, Ransom." Her voice was shy.

Ransom smiled at her, then looked at the debacle of the kitchen.

"I imagine you need to be getting back to the woodshop," Beth said, beginning to wipe down one of the counters.

"And leave you with all this mess?" he demanded. "No way. We'll clean, and then you can come home with me for a cup of tea." He went on when he saw that she hesitated. "You want to have the place looking top-notch for Viola and Rose, don't you? And I know they would want you to thank Mamm for the extra berries."

He was relieved when she nodded her agreement, and then he grabbed a dish towel and went to attack the cookstove with a vengeance.

Beth walked beside him as they passed the Kauffman store, which was the heart of the Ice Mountain Amish community. She glanced briefly at the white store steps, glad that no one was outside, for surely gossip would get back to Viola that she was with Ransom. She held a jar of blueberry sauce to give as a thank-you to Frau King, because she knew that no two blueberry cannings were the same—everyone had their own secrets for flavoring the blueberries.

She eyed Ransom covertly as he walked and wondered for the fourth time why he was taking an interest in her.

"I'm not, you know," he said, smiling faintly.

"Wh–what? Not what?"

"Just being nice to you for some reason or another."

"How did you—I . . ."

"Beth, you have an honest face, and that's a *gut* thing. I want to spend this time with you."

"Why?"

She watched him tilt his head, as if listening to some faerie song only he could hear, but then he turned and smiled at her once more, and she felt her heart begin to throb in her throat.

"You want the truth?" He leaned down close beside her and the sun caught on the dark sheen of his hair.

"*J–jah*," Beth whispered.

He blinked dark lashes and she tried to breathe. "I don't know why."

"What?" Whatever she'd expected him to say, those words were certainly not it.

"Well, I know why," she said on an exhalation. "You–you must feel sorry for me an–and are simply being kind."

He laughed out loud, and she frowned at him. "What did I say?"

He shook his head and straightened, exposing more of his handsome profile. "Nothing. Forgive me. I have an odd sense of humor."

"Oh . . ." She nearly jumped when his large hand covered hers.

"Beth, whatever you said, I wasn't laughing at you. And as for kindness, well, that's not me. Not by a long shot."

Chapter Twelve

Ransom was glad that the turmoil of the morning in his *mamm*'s kitchen had settled down to a mild roar. He didn't blink as he led Beth into the living room from the back door and Old Jack landed on his shoulder.

"Liiike her! Like her!"

"Yes, yes . . ." Ransom muttered and indicated that Beth should sit down on the couch, forgetting that Petunia had claimed that seat as her own. But apparently, the pink pig was willing to share and jumped from the floor to Beth's side to snuggle with contentment.

Ransom started to move Petunia, but Beth shook her head, her blue eyes smiling up at him. "It's fine, Ransom, really."

He backed off and was headed for the kitchen when Matthew, Mark, and Luke passed him in a galloping blur and threw themselves as close to Beth as the couch and Petunia would allow. Aenti Ruth laughed as she came into the room with her cane in one hand and Pig's birdcage in the other.

"My animals are smart, Ransom. Let them be where they are comfortable."

Ransom sighed, then nodded with a sympathetic look toward Beth, who was still serene and poised as she sought to pet everyone.

Esther met him on his way to the sink. "So, you're finally caught bringing a *maedel* home?" His sister's voice was teasing.

"I am not bringing Beth home," Ransom said softly.

"Then why exactly is she sitting under that pile of pig and dog? And Aenti Ruth sure seems to like her, which is remarkable, because Aenti Ruth only likes you. . . ." Esther laughed, and Ransom clenched his jaw.

"Now, now," their mother said. "No arguing. We are glad to have Beth Mast as a guest in our home. I know it's the truth that she rarely has an opportunity to get out."

Ransom raised a dark eyebrow at Esther, who flounced away into the living room. "What are you doing with Beth Mast here?" his *mamm* asked in a whisper. "I've never known you to bring someone home—I mean a girl—even if you aren't bringing her home really."

"I wanted you to give her a cup of tea and take her blueberry sauce and just treat her kindly as a friend of mine," Ransom explained. "Viola and Rose were out—as could be expected on canning day. Still," he mused, "we had fun putting up the blueberries." His *mamm* nodded, apparently satisfied and helped as he unself-consciously set a tea tray. They put together egg salad and cucumber sandwiches on nutty brown bread and Ransom made some licorice tea—one of his favorites. Now and then he paused to listen to Beth's gentle laugh as she talked with Aenti Ruth, and he found the sound to be pleasant to his ears. Then he carried in the tray.

Beth accepted a plate and a cup from the tea tray with true pleasure. It was not often that someone waited on her and she found the moment to be delightful, even though she had to push back the urge to ask if she could help in any way.

Aenti Ruth made a brisk remark halfway through the small meal. "Well, my dear Beth, it seems that the family is fond of you. Matthew, Mark, and Luke have not even tried to beg a crust from you. And, as I've said before, I only wish you could have met John. I still miss him dearly."

"Ach, I know," Beth said with warmth. "I thought of you and prayed for you the other night, thinking about you missing John."

Beth was surprised to see tears glimmer in the old woman's sharp blue eyes. Aenti Ruth cleared her throat.

"Well, my dear, thank you very much. It's not often that young people will take time to think about their elders, especially elders who are being sentimental. So, let's change the subject . . . I bet some of you young folks don't know the folklore surrounding the blueberries we spent so much time picking yesterday."

"Oh, that sounds interesting," Beth said with a smile.

"*Gut.* I'm glad to have your pretty ears, my dear." Aenti Ruth adjusted herself more comfortably in her chair. "The blueberry has what is referred to as a calyx at the top of the berry, and the calyx has five points, which resemble a star. The American Indians called them 'star berries' and believed they flourished in order to provide sustenance for their people. The Native Americans also used the blueberries for medicinal purposes. The roots of the blueberry bush were soaked in hot water and the resulting tea was considered to feed the blood and help to reduce the pain of childbirth."

"I never knew," Beth murmured.

"It's fascinating really," Aenti Ruth said meditatively. "Ransom, are you listening?"

Beth glanced at Ransom, only to find him apparently studying her own person, and she looked away quickly.

Aenti Ruth muttered, "Hmmm. . . . Well, the blueberry juice was also used as a natural dye. The Native Americans made baskets and cloth they wanted to tint and the natural blueberry dye was ideal. Many of the blueberries that were collected ended up being dried and stored. Crushed, dried blueberries were often used as a dry rub for meat."

"Mmm," Beth heard Ransom say with a laugh in his throat. "Blueberry brisket."

Beth swallowed, wondering suddenly with a piercing intensity what it would be like to be married to him and to try out different recipes for his pleasure. It was a tantalizing thought. . . .

Ransom was admiring Beth's profile as some of her shyness melted away and she talked and laughed with Aenti Ruth and Esther. He realized that she was someone to share life's secret joys and laughter with—but then he harshly cut into his own thoughts. . . . *Not for someone like you, Ransom . . . Never again . . .* He shifted when Beth suddenly sat up straight on the couch, nearly dislodging Petunia in the process.

"Ach, my," Beth exclaimed. "I've got to get home before Vi—"

Ransom watched her honest face as she paused, but Aenti Ruth stamped her cane imperiously on the floor. "It's not right that a young *maedel* not be able to *kumme* and *geh* and have a bit of freedom!"

"Ach, *nee*, Aenti Ruth," Beth murmured. "It's my fault. I forgot the time. But, *danki* for the history of the blueberry—I've never heard it before."

Beth got to her feet carefully, seemingly anxious not to upset the animals, and made polite *gutbyes* to everyone. She was walking to the front door, and Ransom realized she had no expectation that he would walk her home, which made him all the more eager to do so. But then he heard the voice begin again inside his soul . . . *Stay away from her . . . You'll only hurt and destroy the goodness she has . . .*

Still, he caught up with her at the door, and she smiled shyly at him.

"I'll walk you back." He kept his voice casual and watched her visibly relax.

"Ach . . . *danki*," she murmured.

They set out through the riotous green of summer and he struggled for a moment to find something to say. After a long pause, as he slowed his steps to match hers, he spoke softly. "So, Aenti Ruth can be quite . . . entertaining."

"Ach, she can indeed," Beth agreed. "You're blessed to have her in your life."

"Well, that's one way of looking at it."

"No, I mean truly . . . Sometimes it's nice to have someone to talk to . . . it can get lonely—"

She broke off, and he slanted her a sideways look. "I'm not in the market for keeping away loneliness, Beth."

He saw her blush, but she shook her head just the same. "Sometimes, do—do you get lonely?"

"Well—" Ransom blew out a short breath. "That's sort of a loaded question. In truth, there have been a lot of times I've, uh, sought out . . . well, never mind. Let's just say that I've tried to get past the loneliness, but I think I deserve it."

"You deserve it?" Her tone was one of amazement.

"Forget I said that."

"*Ne–nee* . . . I want to know why someone like you would ever feel that way."

He laughed wryly. "Someone like me? What delusion are you laboring under, Beth Mast? You think I'm some perfect person? I'm not even whole inside. . . ."

"Wh–what do you mean?"

"Nothing. Just drop it . . ."

He heard her suck in a breath and clenched his jaw, not wanting to see if he'd made her cry. *Idiot . . . why couldn't you keep your mouth shut?*

"Maybe you're not the only one . . ." she murmured.

"What did you say?"

They stopped at the front of her *haus* and he suddenly really wanted to hear her response. But she scampered up the steps and then turned quickly to give him a brisk wave.

He lifted a hand in return, feeling he'd missed something but unable to identify the sensation of loss. He turned around and started back toward home, wondering what she'd meant.

Chapter Thirteen

Beth knew she was being secretive—spending time with Ransom and his family—but she wanted to keep the afternoon to herself and prayed that *Gott* would forgive her for wanting to hurry to get home before Viola and Rose might notice she had gone.

And because Beth knew that Rose and Viola were sure to arrive home anytime, she set about making a *gut* supper for them. She hastily pulled a heavy cast-iron frying pan down from its nail on the wall, then put it on the cookstove. She had the fried potatoes well-seasoned and browning nicely in the pan and idly stood eating the remains of a sweet banana bread when the back door squeaked open.

Beth turned with a ready smile, her heart beating a bit anxiously, and called out a gay greeting.

But Viola had a frown on her face, as did Rose, and Beth felt her heart plummet.

Viola stalked to the clean kitchen table and very carefully drew from behind her back a man's straw hat, which she placed on the old wood.

"A man's hat, Beth. Left on the porch. Do you know who it belongs to?"

Beth wet her lips. *Ransom must have left it by*

mistake . . . "I–I—" She straightened her spine. "It's Ransom King's. He stopped and gave me a hand with the blueberry sauce."

"Indeed?" Viola's eyes glittered and Beth held her breath.

"Well, we must return his hat to him, Rose, mustn't we? Now, Beth, my dear, please come and sit down for a moment while the potatoes cook."

Beth moved with halting steps, feeling anxious at what was coming and slid onto the bench at the table, noting that Rose did the same with a sulky air.

"Beth," Viola began, "I'm afraid I have some bad news."

Beth folded her hands in front of her and looked at Viola, while Rose seemed uninterested.

"*Jah*, Viola?"

"You know that your dear *fater* left us very little money except, of course, for the money we earn on the sheep farm."

Beth nodded, unsure of the feelings she had about who it was who actually did the labor on the farm. *What am I thinking? Uncharitable and mean thoughts about my own family?* But there was some tiny niggle of feeling deep inside her that said perhaps the truth was not always as it appeared. . . .

"Beth, since Rose will most likely marry soon, she will need more things, pretty things, for her hope chest, and we simply do not have the extra money."

"Rose is marrying?" Beth asked in confusion.

"Of course, you silly girl. Why, Ransom King is always seeking her out—it is only a matter of time until he asks to court her! Why, I imagine it was she that he sought today when he stopped in."

"Oh . . ." Beth murmured, her thoughts about Ransom in a turmoil. *Plump fool that I am . . .*

"In any case, I've decided that you shall run a pie stand to sell to the *Englischers* who are staying in the summer cabins over on the far side of Ice Mountain. I've already gained Bishop Umble's approval."

"A—pie stand?" Beth felt her natural shyness cause an ache in her stomach.

"That's what I said—and the profits shall be used for Rose's hope chest. Now, you can begin tomorrow and bake an assortment of pies tonight before bed. You may use the wagon to transport the pies over yonder each morning. I only expect you to work at the stand for a few hours, and then come back to do your normal chores."

"What shall I put the pies on?" Beth asked, beginning to feel swallowed by the amount of work she was expected to achieve each day.

"You and Rose may walk over to the Kings' woodshop and ask if they might *kumme* and put up a little stand—I'm perfectly willing to pay for it, of course."

"*Jah*, Viola," Beth murmured, her usual anxiousness to please her stepmother somehow not quite outweighing her thoughts of work. *Yet, perhaps Gott has given me the extra work to keep my mind from foolishly straying to Ransom . . .*

Ransom was in the woodshop, talking with his *daed*, when Beth and Rose came over in the dusk of the evening. Going outside to greet them, he saw that Beth was holding her hands behind her back while Rose stood primly beside her stepsister, carrying a man's Amish hat.

Great, Ransom thought. *Just great. I left my hat over there and now Beth's family will know I visited her. . . .*

"We're only to stay a few moments, Ransom," Rose said with a faintly simpering frown at Beth. "Mother wanted to see if you might come over to the far side of the mountain tomorrow and build a little pie stand. We need to increase our income, don't we, Beth?"

"*Jah.*" Beth nodded, staring straight ahead.

Ransom felt like wringing Rose's neck when she teasingly put his hat back on his head. He straightened the brim and looked once more at Beth. "And I take it that you will work this pie stand, Beth?"

But before Beth could reply, Rose gave a faint cry and collapsed in a heap on the ground at his feet. He bent automatically to lift her into a sitting position, and Beth scrambled to try to help.

"Ach . . . Rose!"

Beth was very clearly concerned, but even in the fading light, Ransom had seen Rose's eyelids flutter a bit as soon as he'd touched her. So he drew Rose up on wobbly legs, then put a purposeful foot lightly on her right insole.

Rose snapped to a straight stance. "Ouch! Ransom King, you are the clumsiest—I mean, how clumsy of me . . . Ach, Beth, I'm glad you're strong so I can lean on you on the way home."

Ransom resisted the urge to step on her other foot and instead moved close to Beth and caught her chin in his hand, much to his own surprise. "Your—uh—*kapp* string needs straightening." And with gentle fingers, he touched the white string and brushed the soft curve of her cheek. He was aware of both girls' eyes upon him but didn't care at the moment.

He wanted to convey to Beth that he cared for her . . . *That I care for her? What am I thinking? I'd only ruin her life, choke it from her* . . .

He moved his hand from her face and offered his fingers to Rose in a brief salute. "Tell your *mamm* I'll be over there bright and early to set up the stand." He waved them off into the gloaming, cursing hard against his own irrational desire to kiss Beth good night.

"Well, Beth, you are a clever minx," Rose said irritably as they headed out onto the main path.

Beth glanced at her stepsister. "Likely you're still feeling poorly, Rose dear. We'll *geh* home and I'll make you some tea."

"I don't want any tea, but I do want you to know that any interest Ransom King shows in you is based on pity—not feelings of the heart."

Beth swallowed hard to keep the tears from filling her eyes; she resolutely clung to the belief that Rose was overwrought and tired. She didn't want to imagine what Rose meant about pity, though her self-aware mind whispered that it had something to do with her weight.

"You needn't worry, Rose. I don't expect I'll have much time to speak to Ransom in the future, what with the new pie stand and all."

"I was never worried, Beth. Simply pointing out a fact." And Rose flicked irritably at one of Beth's *kapp* strings.

This time, Beth allowed her tears to fall. . . .

* * *

Beth was dreaming, terrorized by the familiar scene playing out before her eyes. Her mind caught each sound, each word, and then she touched her father's arm . . . The horse screaming, the lurching pitch and then she was thrown free . . . always free . . . But I don't want to be . . . I don't want to be. . . . I'm not free inside . . . I deserve to be punished . . . Deserve to be unloved. . . .

Chapter Fourteen

Beth stood alongside the makeshift pie stand and felt perspiration run down her back. She had been up since midnight baking pies, and then, because it was so early and Ransom had not come yet to make her pie stand, she'd tied off Teddy, the family's horse, to a convenient branch, and was prepared to sell out of the back of the wagon. She could see the row of cabins in the near distance and studied them briefly for any sign of awakening. The cabins were rustic, similar in style to the Amish homes but varied in size. Bright swimming towels were hung casually over front porch railings, evidence of creek wading, and fishing rods were also to be seen in abundance. Beth wondered briefly at the lives of the *Englisch* who rented the Amish-owned cabins for the summer months, but then her thoughts turned toward home.

She had not realized that the family's money situation was as bad as Viola had said, and she felt guilty for the faint rumblings of feeling she had inside that said Rose might have gotten up to help bake as well. "You're getting mean, my fine miss," she whispered, waiting for someone to *kumme* to the wagon.

Then a child's plaintive wail cut across the hill

from one of the cabins. Beth saw one of the doors fly open and a harassed-looking woman step out onto the porch. *Kinner* tumbled behind her like so many puppies, and when she saw Beth, she made a beeline straight for the wagon.

Beth listened as the *Englisch* woman practically shouted over the voices of her children. "Do you have any apple pie? They need something for breakfast!"

Beth indicated the three apple pies she had. "I have one lattice top and two with crumb topping."

The woman considered a wad of dollar bills in her hand. "How much are they?"

Beth glanced at the four children and back to the tired-looking mother. "Two for seven or four dollars each."

"I'll take two," the woman decided, smiling with apparent relief at the reasonable cost.

Beth watched them head back across the grass in relative silence now that the *kinner* had the prospect of food and told herself that *Gott* wouldn't mind if she didn't make as much profit on some folks' purchases when her pies could make children happy.

Later, after she had done a rather brisk trade despite her shyness, she had only two pies left—a pecan and a strawberry rhubarb—when she heard a sudden rustling from the narrow path behind her. She tensed, wondering who it might be. She expected that someone Amish would emerge from the woods, but instead, it was a lanky, older *Englischer*, carrying a fishing pole, with a cigarette clamped between his lips. Beth met his eyes and for some reason felt a shiver of fear slide down her back.

The man stopped to grind out the cigarette with a

booted heel directly in front of the makeshift stand and looked down at her with a faint grin.

"Am—ish girl. Kinda pretty too. I'll take that pecan pie."

"Thank you," Beth whispered, feeling her heart begin to pound with nervousness. The cabins across the hill suddenly seemed very quiet and she realized how alone she was.

His grin widened. "Scared as a rabbit, ain't ya?"

Beth thought about running into the woods behind her, but she knew that would not help. The man might follow . . .

She swallowed hard and straightened her spine. "Go away." Her voice came out in a thready squeak and she felt herself begin to shake.

The man laughed, then reached out to put a rough hand on her shoulder. "How's about a little kiss?"

"How about you get going down this mountain before I shove that pie and my fist down your throat?"

Beth jumped and turned at the sound of Ransom's voice. Neither she nor the *Englischer* had heard anyone coming, and Beth saw the Kings' wagon and Benny pulled off some distance behind them.

"Here, now," the *Englischman* said softly. "We wuz only havin' a little fun. I'll take my pie and head out." He picked up the pecan pie and started to walk away.

"Wait!" Ransom's voice snapped like a whip. "Did you pay for that?"

The man turned back around and Beth whispered frantically, "It's all right, Ransom. *Sei se gut . . .*"

"How much is the darn thing?"

"Ten dollars even," Ransom replied.

The man muttered to himself, then pulled two

balled-up bills from his front jeans pocket. He threw them carelessly on the ground and headed toward the tall pines with the pie. Beth listened to the silence after he had gone.

She watched Ransom bend and pick up the money, carefully smoothing it out before he handed it to her. "The—the pies are eight," she whispered.

He lifted his head so she could see the anger on his face. He also looked a bit pale and had a faint, dark shadow along his jaw. "Take the money," he said tightly.

Beth took it, then watched him turn on his heel and head back to his wagon. She fingered the plastic covering of the strawberry rhubarb pie and waited until he'd pulled the wagon into the space near hers, then watched him jump down from the high seat.

He went around to the back of the wagon and started to unload lumber. Beth stood uncertainly, sensing his anger still. "Uh, *danki*, Ransom, for helping me. I—you were wonderful. And that thing you said about your fist and all . . . well, that was a great thing to scare him."

Ransom dropped a two-by-four and stepped close to her, so close she could feel his long legs against the skirt of her dress. She swallowed and looked up at him. "I was dead serious," he bit out. "When I think of what might have happened—*geh* home. *Geh* home, Beth."

"Ach, but I still have one pie to sell," she said with some anxiety.

He gave her a sour smile and pulled out his wallet, withdrew a twenty-dollar bill, and slapped it down on the wagon boards so hard that the strawberry rhubarb jumped. "There. You've sold the last pie."

"I need to give you change."

"Beth . . ."

"*Jah?*"

He drew a deep breath and closed his eyes for a second; then he looked down at her once more. "*Geh* home."

"All right," she agreed. "I'll just get the money box and—"

The sound of a booming thunderclap swallowed her words, and she looked up to see that the dark clouds of a fast-moving storm were directly overhead. The weather seemed to match Ransom's mood, so she nodded at him and started to walk to Teddy and the wagon.

Ransom grabbed Benny's bridle and quickly got the horse unhitched. Then he moved past Beth to do the same for Teddy. The rain was starting to pelt against Ransom's back now, and he took Beth's hand and pulled.

"I can make it home!" she called over the sounds of the rising storm.

"You know Daed has a small barn out here! *Kumme* on!" He ignored her uncertainty and led them through the forest toward the shelter.

It was raining in earnest now, soaking them both. Beth fell once or twice on the slippery roots, but he helped her up each time and bellowed, "Are you all right?" To which she nodded. The horses moved along nicely, for which Ransom was grateful, and he soon caught the latch on the barn door and pulled them all inside.

The sudden drop in noise amplified the sound

of Ransom's own breathing, rough and raw, as he glanced down at Beth's soaked apron and dress. He clenched his jaw when he saw that the wet cotton molded to the outlines of her shoulders. He pulled the horses past her, deeper into the quiet barn his *daed* used as a halfway point for getting furniture down the mountain. He secured the horses, trying to ignore the intimacy of the place. He blew out a breath of frustration, then grabbed a buffing towel from a shelf and went back to Beth, who looked rather like a ruffled little owl. Her *kapp* was on sideways and her dress hung in damp folds about her while she shivered visibly, her arms now hugging her body.

Ransom stripped off his own wet shirt, then moved to gently begin to rub the towel over Beth's hair. Her hidden hairpins gave way, and soon her hair came down in a riotous fall.

"Ach, Ransom," she groaned, covering her face with her hands. "You know it's only a husband who may see a girl's hair unloosed. What am I going to do?"

"Let me finish drying your hair," he said roughly, moving behind her to take off her *kapp*. "Do you want to catch pneumonia? You can bundle the whole thing up again before you *geh* home."

"I'd better hurry on," she whispered. "Viola is likely to be looking for me."

He came around and bent in front of her, carefully prying her hands from her face. She looked at him with a bleak little smile. "Viola will be look—"

"Beth," he broke in softly. "Do you really believe that your stepmother is concerned about where you are?" He let the question hang in the air, staring into her blue eyes, while the rain thrummed on the barn roof.

"I—" Beth wet her lips. "I want to believe that." She swallowed. "I do believe that. Besides, I owe Viola and Rose a great deal—"

"For what? Why do you owe them?" His voice came out harsher than he'd intended, but he kept his eyes locked on hers.

"I owe them." Her bottom lip quivered. "Because they give me a home, and besides—"

"Besides what, Beth? And what the heck kind of a home do they give you? One where you're a servant and have to beg for the smallest privilege, one where that sister of yours rules over you and—"

"Shut up! Just shut up!"

He watched her curl into herself, rocking back and forth while a low, keening cry came from her lips.

"Dear *Gott*, Beth. Forgive me." He felt his own throat tighten, and the urge to cry with her was very great, but instead he simply wrapped his arms around her and rocked her himself. "Shhh . . . shhh . . . little hare . . . it's all right. It's all right."

"*Nee*," she sobbed. "It will never be all right again in my life. You don't understand."

He smiled grimly and murmured low, "You might be surprised."

Then she quieted and lifted her head. Her big eyes were swimming with tears, and one fell over the line of her cheekbone.

"Ach, Beth," Ransom groaned. Then he leaned forward and kissed the track of her tears, which only seemed to make her cry more. Then his mouth found hers and he kissed her without reservation. He slanted his head to deepen the kiss as her novice mouth returned the draw of his lips, and then he pulled away.

He sucked in his breath hard, feeling as though he'd run a mile in a winter's snow. "I'm sorry, Beth. I shouldn't have done that."

She swiped her hands across her cheeks. "*Nee*, I understand."

He studied her carefully. "What do you understand?"

"I—I know that you—um—"

"You should know that I like kissing you," he said abruptly at the warm blush of color that touched her cheeks. He reached out to gently stroke one of the light brown tendrils of hair that brushed the curve of her neck. He very much wanted to kiss her again, but he heard that the rain had slowed and knew that she was in a compromising situation, being alone with him in the barn.

"Best to bundle up your hair and put on your *kapp*," he said with a bit more gruffness than he felt. "The storm is passing and I'd better *geh* back and build you that pie stand."

Beth nodded, hastily lifting her arms and putting up her hair. Then she pinned on her *kapp*. "How does it look?" she asked shyly.

Beautiful. Beautiful . . . "You look nice. Your hair is fine."

She nodded her thanks; then he got to his feet and pulled on his damp shirt and went to get Benny and Teddy. But the whole time he was aware of Beth's presence; the fresh mint smell of her soap and the tender scent of new spring that seemed to cling to her hair. *I am losing my mind,* he told himself.

When he was ready, she reached out and handed

him the strawberry rhubarb pie. "Don't forget," she murmured.

He exhaled slowly. "Believe me—I'll always remember."

He took her arm and led her carefully back out into the fast-breaking sunshine of the early morning.

Chapter Fifteen

Beth went home and gave Viola the pie money, even as she longed to *geh* to her room and think of Ransom. She told herself that she was being silly and set about polishing the loft ladder's wooden staircase. She'd gotten to the fifth step up when it occurred to her that Thumbelina had not *kumme* to greet her upon her return, nor had the cat been anywhere around while she'd been polishing. Worried now, she hastily finished the last few steps, then went in search of Viola.

Her stepmother was sitting in the living room doing some tatting, and Beth had to try hard not to burst out with her worry for her pet. She knew Viola didn't like noisy behavior.

"Beth?" Her stepmother's voice broke into Beth's thoughts.

"*Jah*, Viola."

"You've finished the loft ladder? You may *geh* on with the kitchen floor."

"*Jah*, Viola, I surely will. But I wondered *sei se gut* if you've seen Thumbelina? He doesn't seem to be—"

"*Ach*, that silly cat," Viola replied dismissively.

"When the storm came earlier today, I opened the back door and the animal ran outside."

Beth's heart began to pound. "But Thumbelina is usually wherever I am around the *haus*. He may be lost or hurt or—"

"You needn't fuss at me, Beth. *Geh*—" Viola waved a magnanimous hand. "*Geh.* You may have an hour free to look for the cat. But be back in one hour; there are chores waiting."

"*Jah*, Viola. *Danki.*"

Beth walked quietly away, knowing if she hurried, she'd only be called back. But once out of earshot of her stepmother, Beth ran out the back door and began to anxiously call for Thumbelina.

Her search seemed futile, but when she'd gone about half a mile from the *haus*, she nearly tripped over a gray sack on the ground. She might have gone on, except she heard a frail whimper come from inside the bag. Quickly, she bent and opened the sack, only to find a very small puppy inside. He looked malnourished and as though he'd been kicked around. His back legs were tied together so he couldn't run, and his eyes seemed to plead with her for help.

"Ach, you poor thing." She knelt down on the ground and tried to work at the string that was cutting into the animal's legs, but she had no pocketknife and couldn't get it to loosen with her short nails.

Then the clear sound of wood being hammered came to her in the distance, and she remembered that Ransom was probably still working on the pie stand and was not all that far away. She got to her feet with the puppy and started to run down the dirt road that would lead out to the pie stand.

Ransom turned to pick up a nail and saw Beth running down the path toward him. He immediately put down his hammer, pocketed the nail, and set out to meet her. His long legs covered the ground much more quickly than Beth's, and she soon thrust the puppy into his arms with a sob. "Ach, Ransom, I can't get the string off his legs. I found him in a sack along the way. And Thumbelina is missing too!"

Ransom decided to tackle the most pressing of her concerns first. Putting one arm around her and carrying the puppy with the other, he led her back to the pie stand, which was almost finished, only needing a shade roof. He put the puppy down on the fresh pine wood and, using his pocketknife, very carefully cut the tight string, then rubbed the legs of the poor animal to bring back some circulation.

"Do you think he's badly hurt?" Beth asked.

Ransom ran careful hands over the animal and shook his head. "No bones broken. He's half-starved and has been treated badly, but I do think he'll pull through all right."

"Ach, I wish I could take him home, but Viola forbids any dogs because of their barking."

"I'll have him," Ransom said, lifting the animal to cuddle against his chest.

"Ach, but maybe I have a better idea," Beth exclaimed.

"What's that?"

"Let's give him to Aenti Ruth. . . . You know . . . Matthew, Mark, Luke, and well—Second John!"

Ransom laughed heartily. "All right! Let's take him over in the wagon right now."

"I can't," Beth groaned. "I have to find Thumbelina and I have less than an hour before I have to get back."

"It will only take a few minutes to give the pup to Aenti Ruth, and then I'll help you look for Thumbelina."

He watched Beth consider, and the puppy whimpered. "Ach, *jah*! Let's *geh*!" she burst out.

They entered the *haus* to the usual cacophony of animal sounds that had become commonplace since Aenti Ruth's arrival. The *auld* lady sat upright in the chair she'd come to favor and Ransom let Beth approach with the puppy.

"I found him, Aenti Ruth," Beth whispered. "He looks quite a mess now, but I'm sure he'll grow into a fine-looking friend. And I thought you might call him Second John."

Aenti Ruth's hands shook a bit as she reached out for the small dog. "My—I—don't quite know what to say. I—*danki*, child. Of course he shall be fine. Ransom King, don't just stand there—fetch some warm milk . . . ach, and send Jack in."

Aenti Ruth's blue eyes gleamed. "Something tells me that I may have a gift for you too, little Beth."

Beth looked up in time to see Thumbelina come sauntering in with Jack the parrot riding on his sleek back. The two seemed to be the firmest of friends, and when Beth ran to meet her beloved pet, Thumbelina purred in happy greeting. "Oh, how did you find him?"

"I figured he belonged to someone hereabouts as he was in such good condition," Aenti Ruth said. "And I didn't find him—he came scratching at the door in the middle of the storm. Smart cat, I say!"

"Ach, *jah, danki*. He is."

Beth perched on the edge of the sofa, trying to decide how best to take her leave without seeming impolite when Aenti Ruth cleared her throat, then spoke low. "Dear child, *Derr Herr* prompts me to give you one more thing. A secret thing. One I have carried with me for nigh on three generations now. Hand me my Bible."

Beth would have protested that it was unnecessary, but there was a spark of light in Aenti Ruth's eyes that made Beth feel she should obey.

Beth handed her the heavy Bible, filled with notes, cards, and ribbons to mark special readings. Aenti Ruth managed the puppy and the Bible easily in her lap, then opened the pages to begin to hunt for something in particular. Beth waited, outwardly patient but inside fearing repercussions if she didn't make it home within the allotted time. But suddenly Aenti Ruth drew a recipe card from the center of the Bible.

"Had it in Job. Praise be. Here, Beth. Take it, but guard it well."

Beth looked down at the simple card with its old-fashioned, beautiful handwriting. "Ach, thank you, but I—"

"You will know when to use it."

Beth nodded, not really understanding but not wanting to give offense.

Aenti Ruth gestured with an aged hand. "Quickly, hide it away and let no one else use it."

Beth carefully put the recipe card into her dress pocket as Ransom came in with a small bottle of warmed milk.

"Excellent." Aenti Ruth's voice rose. "Now, I will feed Second John and you, Ransom, can have the privilege of taking Beth and her smart cat home."

Beth bent and kissed the *auld* woman, who in turn patted her cheek and whispered in Beth's ear, "Remember."

Ransom was dreaming, surrounded by sparkling water as he leaped in the ocean with the moon shining down on him. Then the moon was gone and Barbara was driving the automobile, going much too fast and then faster still. Maybe this was dying—out of control—flying, dying . . . He heard his own choked breath, pulling him back to wakefulness. . . .

He sat up in bed and looked out of the window. A summer moon shone down peacefully, and the fresh smell of blooming things wafted in from outside. He was home—on Ice Mountain—the dream was over, but he knew he still wouldn't sleep. Instead, he lay back and flung an arm over his eyes, trying to control his breathing. Soon he was less tense but just as stirred up when visions of Beth and ripe blueberries began to tease his mind.

Chapter Sixteen

Beth had nearly forgotten about the recipe card Aenti Ruth had given her until the next morning, when she was dressing. She went to the peg on the wall where she'd hung her apron the *nacht* before and felt carefully in the pocket. She withdrew the aged card and glanced through the ingredients— one of them surprised her but made her smile. Then she recalled that Aenti Ruth had wanted her to hide the card, and she went to the wooden dresser that her *fater* had bought her from an *auld* Amish craftsman. She drew in a deep breath and lifted a cleverly concealed piece of scrollwork to reveal a hidden compartment. Her eyes welled with tears as she remembered her *daed* leaving little notes for her in the secret place; she knew that not even Viola was aware of the hiding place. Quickly, she folded the recipe card in half and slipped it into the hollow space, then closed the scrollwork and stepped away.

It was so difficult to touch anything that reminded her of her father, for theirs had been a cheerful and loving relationship and he had always been her protector against the world. She remembered especially their appreciation of the beauty of Ice Mountain and how her *daed* would often take her to search for the creatures *Gott* had made on the mountain. Once, he'd taken her fishing and they'd *kumme* upon a baby fawn, hiding in the tall grass beside the creek. Beth had wanted very much to take the sweet thing home.

"*Nee*, my dear. The fawn is hiding and waiting for its *mamm* to return. The mama deer would be quite unhappy to find its baby missing." He'd rubbed her hand in consolation, and Beth remembered smiling as she looked up into her *daed*'s kind eyes.

"Would you miss me, Da, if you found I'd disappeared?"

Her *fater* had hugged her close. "My very heart would break, little love."

Beth had been satisfied with his answer and they'd gone on to take one last peek at the fawn and then spent a *gut* afternoon fishing.

Now Beth put aside such happy thoughts with a sigh and left her room to climb down the ladder. She grabbed two corn muffins as she passed through the silent kitchen and ate them on the way out to check on Cleo, her lambs, and the rest of the sheep.

Beth lit a lantern inside the barn and peered over the small stall at Cleo. Immediately, Beth could tell the sheep was distressed. It was an instinctive knowledge and she put down the lantern on a barrel top and slipped inside the stall. The lambs were curled up asleep next to one another, but Cleo stood still. Beth knelt down in the hay and felt Cleo's udder, knowing already that she would find it hot to the touch.

"Mastitis, Cleo, and a bad case. We'll have to have Bishop Umble out as soon as possible. It will be fine." Bishop Umble had been a shepherd when he was first married to Martha, long years ago. And he was still an expert on animal husbandry. Beth told herself that she was reassuring the sheep, but, in fact, she was also comforting herself. She knew that mastitis could be dangerous to a sheep and also to her lambs, because the condition made it too painful for the ewe to nurse her babies.

Beth picked up the lantern and hurried out of the barn. The bishop and his wife lived quite near the mountain store, and she knew she could reach him faster on foot than by hitching up Teddy. Most likely, the bishop was at Ben Kauffman's store anyway, for an early morning round of checkers.

All of this went through Beth's mind in an instant as she walked the dirt path to the big white store. She intended to check inside before going on to Martha's *haus* and she climbed the stairs quickly. She went inside and was met by the familiar sights and delicious aromas that accompanied each trip to the well-lit space. She saw the gathering of Amish men in the back aisle and quickly made her way over the hardwood floor, her normal shyness lost in the urgency she felt for Cleo.

She explained the situation, and Bishop Umble promised to be there within the half hour, so she walked back to the barn and paced outside. When she saw the pinkish purple streaks of dawn cross the sky, she wondered vaguely what Ransom was doing at that hour. Then Bishop Umble came whistling down the lane and she walked over with the light to greet him.

"Beth, so it's Cleo, is it?" he asked, already in his shirtsleeves.

"*Jah*, but I think we caught it early."

The *auld* man did a quick examination, then drew some fluid from the teat. "I heard Ransom King gave you a hand with the delivery. The lambs look well hydrated, in any case."

"Um . . . *jah*, Ransom helped."

She didn't miss the assessing glance the bishop shot at her and felt herself flush.

"I see. . . . *Gut* man, Ransom."

"Yes, he is," she replied, feeling out of her depth.

"Well, I'll take this fluid back to the house and have a look. We'll decide which antibiotic to use then. I'll be back out in a few hours."

"*Danki*, Bishop Umble," she murmured.

"Good morning, Beth."

She held the lantern so he could take his leave, then walked back into the *haus*. It was time to start breakfast and get her pies in order for the stand.

Ransom woke late, which was completely unlike himself, but he was glad he'd only dreamed fitfully and not progressed to the sheer panic that often kept him awake all night. He pulled on a dark blue shirt and slipped up his suspenders. He drew a yellow-lined sheet of paper from his dresser drawer and read over the ad he'd sketched out to advertise that the family woodworking shop would be expanding to include fine furniture. He'd already met with his *fater* and the bishop to gain their permission for the plan, and he was especially excited about making it known that the King family was taking a step forward into developing a broader business range.

He went out to where Esther was cooking blueberry

pancakes. "How many do you want?" she asked pointedly.

He *bussed* her quickly on the cheek before she could swat him away, then laughed as he poured his coffee.

"What's got you in such a good mood?" Esther asked.

"Going into Coudersport . . . to set out the advertisement that the King family is expanding,"

"Well—" Esther grinned mischievously. "Mind you don't stop and buy any more pies from Beth Mast. Mamm and I have made enough to last for weeks."

"Beth can bake," he said with a raised brow.

"Uh-huh."

He smiled and swallowed down his coffee, then headed out to the barn to get Benny. His brother Abel was hanging around the barn door, obviously wanting to talk to him.

"Abel, what's going on?"

"Well . . . uh . . . can we *geh* for a walk a ways? I don't want Daed to hear."

"Sure."

Ransom walked quietly beside his *bruder* and couldn't help the feeling of fear that seemed to bite at the back of his neck.

"What is it, Abel?" he asked quietly as they neared the property's pond.

"You know the other *nacht*, when you gave me that money for—"

"*Jah.*"

"Well, how do you know when it's the right time to—do that?" Abel finished lamely.

Ransom swallowed hard. "You—might wait until you're married."

Abel shot him a bleak look and Ransom blew out a tight breath. "All right . . . I can't tell you when, but you better be darn sure before you make—a mistake."

"Well, when did you—uh—first—you know?"

Ransom shook his head, lost in a nightmare in the broad light of day. "Look, Abel—" He heard himself form the words, but it didn't sound like his voice. *I'm a coward*, he thought. "Just pray about it."

"Pray about it? Really?"

At least the kid doesn't sound defensive . . . "Yeah . . . pray hard."

Abel shrugged. "Okay."

Ransom turned on the far side of the pond and they headed back in silence, even as Ransom felt a roaring in his ears.

He felt the jolt of impact and heard Barbara screaming. He tried to reach her, but his hands found hard metal instead, slick with some wet substance. . . .

He blinked in the sunlight and realized that Abel was still speaking to him. Unable to find his voice, he left his younger *bruder* to walk away alone.

Beth had seen the bishop off for the second time that morning and was comforted by the fact that Cleo was on a strong antibiotic. Beth paused now as she saw her blurred reflection in the pail of water she had carried outside to water the other sheep before she went to the pie stand. She stood alone, trapped by the sudden knowledge that she hated her reflection. *Round-faced sinner, never loved, sad and so very broken . . . I don't deserve forgiveness or love, and I don't believe that Gott loves me personally. . . .*

The dangerous train of her thoughts was broken by Rose's critical voice.

"Why are you just standing there? I don't know what gets into your head sometimes."

Beth drew a deep breath and turned to her stepsister. "Rose?"

"What?"

"Do you . . . love me?"

The air hummed with the question as Rose slowly scowled. "Now I know you're *narrisch*, Beth. What kind of question is that?"

Beth stood trembling as she watched Rose turn and go. *I knew what she'd say . . . I knew it would hurt my heart, but I wanted to punish myself for being alive. . . . I wanted to suffer. . . .*

She bent her shoulders forward and automatically finished the watering. Then she went inside the *haus* to wash her hands and pack up the pies.

Chapter Seventeen

Ransom sat bleakly staring out of the buggy as Benny ambled along. The conversation with Abel had shaken him in more ways than one. *If only someone had talked that way to me . . .*

He was so absorbed in his difficult thoughts that he almost didn't realize how far he'd traveled until he came upon Beth setting out the pies for the morning's sale. Her shy smile as he was about to pass was enough to make him hesitate, and his eyes focused on the light green dress she was wearing. There was something restful about her, even though her shyness sometimes made conversing with her difficult.

"*Gut* morning," he said, a smile coming to his lips.

"Hello," she murmured.

"Listen," he said, before he realized the words were even out of his mouth. "I'm in the mood to hike down the mountain and have a breath of air from the Ice Mine."

"*Jah?*" she said slowly, her brow wrinkling in question.

"Well, how about we leave the pies here on the honor system."

"You mean, let people pay themselves and take their own change?"

Ransom nodded. "You'll probably sell just the same and I'll have you back up the mountain before Viola even knows you're gone."

He waited a few moments, his heart thrumming in his ears as he realized how hasty his idea sounded, but Beth didn't answer.

Finally, though, he heard a single soft word. "Why?" she asked.

"Why what?" He took a step nearer to her.

"Why do you want to spend time with me?"

"Beth, I don't know—I told you—I like you, we could be—friends." The word sounded like what it was—thin. He hadn't planned on saying it and, in truth, wished he might take it back, because he suddenly knew in his soul that he loved her. But Beth's gentle features seemed to take on a beautiful hue as she tested the word on her tongue. "Friends?"

He nodded, then looked at the ground. "I should warn you maybe—I'm not what you'd call good friend material."

She smiled rather sadly then. "Perhaps the same could be said of me."

As they walked, Beth glanced at his handsome profile and firm lips and tried to recall his mouth touching hers. It seemed a kindled flame of a memory, and she kept stealing brief looks at him.

"What is it?" he asked.

"Ach, nothing—I was just remembering . . . I mean—" She felt her words become glue in her mouth and paused in defeat.

But he half-smiled and his dark eyes seemed to drink her in as he turned to look her way. "Remembering that kiss?" he asked.

"Ach, no—I mean, how did you know?"

She saw him look back to the mountain trail. "I remember it too. It's kind of hard to forget. You have a mouth that was made for kissing, Beth Mast— strictly speaking as an observant friend, of course."

"Of course," she returned. But then, all the insecurities and self-loathing she'd felt that morning came flooding into her mind.

If he only knew the real me—or what's left of me—he'd never want to be my friend. He'd probably think I'm narrisch *or even worse. And I am worse, because I choose to be . . . I might have the power to be a* gut *friend, one who could help and build and dream, but I know I don't deserve any of it. And I . . .*

She nearly jumped when Ransom caught her hand.

"Watch out for those exposed roots," he cautioned.

Beth looked at the twined root structure of a tall pine, even as she thrilled to the steady strength of Ransom's fingers fitting easily through her own. Was this friendship then? she wondered.

As they walked, Beth felt the heat of the summer's day give way to a subtle coolness around her feet, and she glanced at the bright green ferns that began to pepper their way on the mountain descent.

"How long has it been since you've been to the mine?"

Beth glanced up at him shyly. "Too long," she admitted. "I haven't been off the mountain in a *gut* long while."

He nodded. "I haven't been to the mine in years, though I heard that an *Englischer* is going to open it up for tours once more."

The Ice Mine that sat at the base of Ice Mountain had been discovered accidentally when a miner who'd been seeking silver found beautiful summer ice instead. The curious thing about the mine was that it was filled with ice during the summer but completely bare and temperate in the winter. The Amish saw it as an example of *Gott*'s Provision, while the *Englisch* over the past hundred years had toured the mine in fascination, and while ownership passed from one to another.

"Do you remember the story of the ferns hereabouts?" Beth asked, seeking something to say.

"That they won't survive anywhere else, nor will they grow and take root anyplace but Ice Mountain?" He swung her hand a bit. "Fanciful, isn't it?"

"*Jah*, my *fater* used to tell me that the ferns grew in *Gott*'s Footprints when He trod up Ice Mountain for the first time." She wanted to say more, but this brief revelation about her *fater* brought her pain and she swallowed her words.

"You don't like to talk about him much, do you?"

Beth shook her head, hoping Ransom would let the topic of her earthly *fater geh* by. She was surprised when he stopped on the trail and swung her around so the sunlight that filtered through the tall trees made her blink.

"What is it?" she asked softly, lifting her head to look up into his dark eyes.

"We're alike, you and me, little hare."

She shook her head. "How can you say that when you're so beautiful and I'm . . . well, you know . . ."

"What do I know?"

She frowned, not quite able to say the words that hovered anxiously on her lips.

He slid his big hands up the length of her arms, and she shivered involuntarily. His fingers began to caress the plumpness of her shoulders and she felt as though a wash of warm butter was running down her spine. Her impulse was to pull away, but instead, she made a small sound of pleasure when his hands came up to cup her cheeks and massage behind her ears.

She scrunched her eyes closed and drew a deep breath. "You know that I'm—fat."

He stepped closer to her, his hands still gentling her face, and he bent very near to whisper in her ear. "Fat, little hare? Is that what you think? The secret you hold?"

She swallowed, wondering vaguely what he'd think if he knew her real secret, but then she was lost in the moment, as his mouth came down on hers, gentle but fast.

Ransom knew that what he was doing was out of bounds, but he couldn't help himself. He kissed her, then muttered words into her shell-like ear, wanting her to know how very much he desired her.

"Ach, little Beth, do you know how many sharp edges there are in the world? Your body was made to cradle a man and I love the way you—curve." His lips found hers once more, and he impulsively deepened the kiss, gently exploring her pearly teeth with the tip of his tongue. Then he begged quietly, "Open for me, little hare." He caught the awkward hiccup of air that she exhaled, and he realized she'd never kissed before. The thought both delighted and humbled him.

When he finally pulled away, he was shaken and ran nervous fingers through his hair; then he caught her hand in his once more and continued their descent. He felt out of his depth, so lulled by the ethereal magic of Ice Mountain that, for once, he didn't think of Barbara.

They emerged at the bottom of the trail, and Ransom blinked in the bright sunlight as he helped Beth down the last few steps. The magic spell was broken when he glanced around and spotted a tall *Englischer* striding toward them from what used to be the mine's gift shop.

"Good morning!" The *Englischer*'s voice was hearty and seemed to match his dark red hair and brawny good looks.

Ransom answered politely. "*Gut* morning."

"I'm Ryan Mason."

Ransom shook the other man's hand. "Ransom King and Beth Mast."

Ransom wasn't entirely sure what the man wanted but knew that *Englischers* were sometimes fascinated by the Amish; he wasn't in the mood to be a novelty.

The *Englischer* must have sensed some of Ransom's reserve because he was quick to step away. "You came down to visit the mine, right? Please go on ahead. I just bought the gift shop here and am looking over things. I'm a youth pastor in Coudersport."

Ransom nodded and steered Beth away toward the heavy oaken door that shielded the entrance to the mine. He couldn't really think about anything more than kissing her again and was glad when he found the heavy padlock on the door undone.

"Watch your step," he cautioned as he eased open the door. A blast of cold air greeted them, and then they were swallowed in thick darkness until Ransom turned up the lantern hanging on the cold wall inside.

Beth had forgotten how beautiful the palatial display of summer ice could be. Icicles, some as thick as a man's forearm, hung in a delightful, crystalline cascade. Ransom kept an arm about her waist as they inched forward, careful to avoid the steep drop of the mine shaft itself.

"It's like a bit of heaven, isn't it?" Beth asked, amazed as always by the wonder *Gott* had made.

"*Jah*," Ransom answered throatily. "A bit of heaven."

She felt the breadth of his chest press against her back, and she turned against his arm to look up into his dark eyes, which were illuminated by the lantern light. "You—you're not talking about the ice, are you?"

He shook his head slowly. "*Nee*." Then he bent to press his mouth against the line of her throat. She arched like a contented feline, letting his kisses fall where they might.

"I–I don't know how to kiss right," she murmured. She felt him smile against her lips.

"I'll teach you," he promised.

She felt as though some of the ice had melted around her at his husky words, but then she recalled the world atop the mountain and broke free from him in confusion.

"What is it?" he asked, raising the lantern higher. "You must be careful of your step."

"*Sei se gut,* Ransom—can we *geh* now? I–I'm cold."

"Then let me warm you." He took a step closer, but she drew away. "Little hare, what's wrong?"

"Don't you see?" she pleaded, feeling a single tear trail down her cheek. "When we *geh* back—to Viola and Rose and everybody—you won't—you won't want this—me."

"Viola," he snapped softly. "That's where your thoughts are? Well, then, let us *geh.* I see I'm in need of kissing practice myself."

Beth felt her heart sink. "Please don't be offended." She touched his arm with tentative fingers and saw him give her a rueful smile.

"I suppose I am acting like a fool. *Kumme.* Let's *geh* out and see if that *Englischer* has any ice cream to buy."

Beth smiled and then laughed for a moment of joy as he swiped her mouth with a quick kiss.

Chapter Eighteen

Ransom closed the heavy oak door to the mine, and the first thing he noticed outside was that the air hung heavy with the smell of smoke.

The *Englischer*, Ryan Mason, gestured to them and then pointed to the top of Ice Mountain.

"Fire!" he called. "Looks like it's uncontained."

Ransom grabbed Beth's hand. "It's the *Englisch* cabins, I think, but . . ." He stopped, not wanting to voice the fear he could plainly read on Beth's face—the forest land that grew near the cabins might catch fire as well, and that was a step too near the Amish community.

"*Kumme.*" He hurried with her to the path and was surprised when Ryan joined them.

"You're going to need all the manpower you can get," the *Englischer* offered, and Ransom nodded in agreement as he helped Beth begin the trek up the mountainside.

By the time they reached the top, acrid smoke clung to their hair and clothes and stung their eyes. The *Englisch* cabins were engulfed in flame and bewildered-looking summer campers stood far back from the structures' stark outlines. Ransom saw that many of the Amish men had formed a bucket brigade from the nearby creek and he readily joined in after assuring himself that Beth had headed back to where the Amish women were probably preparing food. Ransom and the *Englischer*, Ryan, ran to the end of the brigade and began working as fast as they could.

The summer breezes were against them and the effort to contain the flames was exhausting, but finally the fire was out and both *Englisch* and Amish staggered together through the woods and back to the Amish community.

Beth half-expected Viola and Rose not to be present among the swirling group of women who were making soup in huge kettles and assembling sandwiches at a stout table. But her stepmother and Rose were moving carefully past the kettles, adding touches of salt and pepper.

Martha Umble, the bishop's wife, kept everything running smoothly and brushed past Beth with a thin elbow.

"If you'd start some bacon corn chowder over with Mary Lyons, Beth, it would be an especial help. Ben Loftus has opened the store for anything we may need."

Beth nodded and made her way to where beautiful Mary Lyons, the schoolteacher's wife, was hastily adding chopped potatoes to a large kettle where crisped and chopped bacon was already sizzling with a rich aroma.

Beth smiled in greeting, then washed her hands with lye soap in a nearby water bucket. She began husking sweet corn, then cutting the milky white kernels off with a heavy knife and dropping them into the kettle.

Mary added several quarts of canned tomatoes and a jar of rich cream. "Now it only needs to heat until the potatoes are cooked through." The older woman touched Beth's hand in thanks for her help.

"*Jah*, I hope the men and *buwes* are safe, and the *Englischers* too . . ." Beth trailed off, recalling that Mary's husband, Jude, had once been *Englisch*.

Mary smiled. "I've come to realize, Beth, that people are people, be they Amish or *Englisch*."

"Of course," Beth murmured. "I'm sorry if I made them sound like an afterthought."

"You didn't," Mary insisted, continuing to smile. "And here *kumme* the men and the folks from the cabins now. They'll be plenty hungry, I imagine. *Ach*, and Ransom King looks as though he's hurt his hand."

Beth's lips parted with the fleeting thought that Mary must know something about Ransom's attentions to her, but then she quickly moved to his side, not even backing off when Rose met him too.

"*Ach*, Ransom . . . what happened? Let me tend you." Rose fluttered about like a beautiful moth, and Beth felt the unkind desire to roll her eyes.

She saw the tight lines of pain around Ransom's mouth and knew that it was no time for silliness. She met Rose's piercing gaze with one of her own and was about to speak when Bishop Umble stopped near them.

"*Ach*, Ransom—I heard you were burned pulling that spaniel out of harm's way. Beth, will you take Ransom over to the healer's cabin while Rose goes back to her *mamm?* I'm sure there's—ah—more salting and peppering to do."

For once, Beth knew a strange feeling of victory, though she understood she'd probably regret it later. Rose flounced off, obviously not daring to contradict the spiritual leader of Ice Mountain.

Beth turned now to peer up into Ransom's face. "Do you want me to *geh* with you to Sarah's?"

She watched his mouth curve in a faint smile, despite the obvious pain he was experiencing. "You know I do."

She felt herself flush at his words, then glanced around to discover they seemed conspicuously paired off—in much the same way that many other couples were, as women helped tend to the small hurts of their men.

She was left with little time for embarrassment, though when she saw that the *Englischer*, Ryan Mason, had a gash on his sooty forehead.

"Ach, you must *kumme* to the healer's cabin," Beth said, calmly touching him on the arm.

"If it means going with you," he agreed, grinning good-naturedly.

Beth saw Ransom's frown but was too intent on getting both men the help they needed to mind.

"Sarah's out right now," Edward King said in his deep voice. The big Amishman looked more pirate than planter with his black eyepatch taut across his strong face. Two small children clung to his legs as he widened the door to the healer's cabin. "Beth, you're welcome to *kumme* in and use what supplies you will. Sarah won't mind. She's still tending to the *Englischers* who were hurt in the fire."

Ransom watched Beth give a shy nod of acknowledgment as she brushed past Edward and entered the noisy fray of the kitchen. Children dotted the place like wild sprites, and Ransom had to sidestep the *kinner* more than once, but it pleased him to see Beth smile at the children and move confidently among them.

She'd make an excellent mamm . . . *gentle, kind* . . . He had to shake himself from the gleaming thought of her and only refocused when she gently lifted the cloth from the burn on his arm. He heard her suck in her breath.

"Ach, Ransom, it's nasty."

"It'll be fine," he said roughly, not wanting to notice how much her tender touch affected him as her fingers skimmed the edges of the wound.

"We can put some balm on it and dress it lightly until Sarah returns." Beth looked up at him for approval. He nodded, watching her move with confidence. Here was a side he didn't know she possessed—a knowledge of healing as well as baking . . . *and kissing,* his mind whispered with charged intent. He set his jaw and focused on his wound and was soon dispatched to sit in one of the kitchen chairs while a little *maedel* clambered onto his lap. Edward and Sarah King were nothing if not fruitful. . . .

"*Sei se gut,* Ryan, please sit down and I'll try to clean up your forehead." Ransom felt himself frown darkly as she moved to touch the visibly smitten *Englischer.*

But Ryan was cheerful and pleasant to talk with,

and Ransom soon found himself reluctantly liking the fellow.

"I've heard you apprenticed in fine furniture making," Ryan said as Beth dabbed at his forehead.

Ransom raised an eyebrow. "How did you hear that? I've only been home a short while and haven't had time to advertise."

The *Englischer* smiled. "Oh, things get around. . . ."

"I just met you . . ." Ransom felt an acceleration in his heart rate. This Ryan reminded him of Bishop Umble in his weird knowing of things.

"Oh, well." Ryan nodded. "If you do such work, I was thinking that you might display your craft in rebuilding the cabins."

Ransom shifted the child's slight weight in his arms and enjoyed a throttling hug from the skinny arms of the little girl. When he could breathe, he nodded at Ryan. "It's a *gut* idea. I would imagine that some folks lost a lot in the fire because most of them stay for the whole summer."

Ransom caught Beth's smile as she said, "Ach, Ransom, it would be wonderful to see your work. I know so little of your time with your *grossdauddi* . . ."

He swallowed as memories suddenly seeped through his mind—Barbara had been interested in his work—or so she had said . . . He snapped back to the present as Ryan continued speaking.

"Actually, I know there's a pastor's wife and kids who are up here on sabbatical—the pastor had a heart attack and died. He was young—thirty-eight, I believe . . . the church just wanted them to have a chance to heal, but now . . . with the fire . . ."

Ransom felt his interest grow. "I'll talk to my *daed*. It would be *gut* to help them out."

He realized that the place had quieted as gentle Sarah returned with a quick *buss* on Edward's mouth and a smile for her patients.

"You did wonderfully, Beth," the older girl praised. "Let me know if you ever need something more to do. I could use an assistant."

Ransom knew a glimmer of joy to see the shy smile of pleasure on Beth's face.

Chapter Nineteen

"But Bishop Umble told me to help Ransom, Viola, and think what good it would do to help the *Englischers*. . . ."

"Help the *Englischers*! Why, if you haven't enough work to do here, Beth, in support of your own family—I just don't know what to say."

Beth bit her lip and scooped up Thumbelina. She walked away quietly and climbed the ladder to her own room, even though it was nearly stifling in the middle of the day. She just wanted a few moments to be alone after listening to Viola for nearly half an hour. She realized that this desire to be by herself bordered on the disobedient, but she knew she would go back down soon enough.

She also realized that she was hungry and rummaged in a tin for some raisin cookies that were half stale but still sweet. She chewed thoughtfully and had a sudden memory of sitting down to dinner with her father for meals. Now, she usually served Viola and Rose and was kept hopping up and down. Besides, she didn't want to sit with anyone. She felt a lot safer going to her room and eating alone. She felt more in control and she didn't have to be still and listen to the echoes within herself that she tended to hear more loudly when she was with others—like Viola and Rose.

From her screened window, she heard a horse and buggy come along the dirt lane. She glanced out, wondering if it might be Ransom for some reason. But she saw Bishop Umble's wife, Martha, climb out of the buggy, and she hastened to tidy herself and *geh* back downstairs.

Martha Umble was a kind soul who made the rounds visiting and praying with the women of the community. Viola always seemed flustered by the older woman and Beth was never quite sure why.

But, as Beth served the ladies iced tea with fresh mint, she was surprised to hear that Martha was already talking about Olivia Lott and her family. All of the other summer renters had left the mountain, but Olivia had no place to *geh* with the death of her husband. Ransom must have spoken to the bishop, and here was his wife already helping to find support for the project. The Amish grapevine, Beth thought, and helped herself to a quick sip of tea as she listened to the conversation.

"And, of course, Viola, I must thank you for allowing Beth to be part of this, because she and Ransom were the ones to see the need in the first place."

Beth held her breath a bit, wondering what her stepmother might say. But Viola seemed to rise to the occasion. "Why, surely Beth must help. We all must, right, Rose?"

"Oh, *jah*," Rose murmured vaguely.

Beth felt satisfied that even though it might be through the subtle pressure of the bishop's wife, she would be able to participate. And further, she saw for the first time, with some clarity, that Viola wanted to be accepted. *Maybe that's why she seems angry much of the time . . .*

But this was just the glimmer of a thought, quickly forgotten in the flurry of the activity Viola galvanized once Martha Umble had gone.

Beth wondered briefly what Ransom was doing, but dragged her mind from him and tried to focus on the tasks at hand.

Ransom let his mind drift over the day and knew in his heart that the hike down the mountain with Beth had changed him somehow. He felt with growing certainty that his injured soul had healed a bit in the light of Beth's gentleness.

Gott said, *"Perfect love, whole love, casts out fear . . ." How would it feel to no longer be afraid of what I've done? Is that even possible?*

The hard thoughts were difficult to contemplate. . . .

At least his talk with Bishop Umble had gone well. The community's spiritual leader was kind and generous and had a *gut* relationship with the *Englisch* of the area. He had told Ransom he would get the word around the community that the rebuilding of the cabins was both a *gut* idea and a *gut* ministry.

Beth was tired, but nonetheless, she tossed and turned in her hot room, unable to get comfortable. She finally grabbed a pillow and quilt and decided to *geh* down to the back porch to sit in the coolness of the *nacht* for a bit. She stopped in the kitchen and grabbed half a chocolate cream pie and a fork, then tiptoed outside with Thumbelina accompanying her.

The stars were burning brightly against the midnight-blue sky, and the moonglow lit the kitchen garden so that she could even see the tomatoes on the bushes, looking silvery and shadowed. She sat down in a wicker-backed chair and tucked up her legs under her, adjusting the quilt and taking her first forkful of pie. She savored its sweetness, her satisfaction intensified because the pie was being eaten in secret. She thought about this as she licked the back of the fork and knew she had never eaten in secret when she was younger. The habit had grown since her *fater*'s death. The more she could hide when she ate and how much, the more in control she felt. She knew this left little room for what *Gott* commanded—to love your neighbor as yourself. *How can I love anyone when I can't love myself?* she wondered. She thought briefly of Ransom, a flare against the dark of her mind, then nearly jumped when Jack the parrot flew onto the porch and landed on top of Thumbelina. She put down the pie plate on the porch floor and welcomed the bird. But then she wondered if Aenti Ruth would be troubled by Jack's absence.

She sighed to herself, knowing she'd have to take him back, and quickly went inside to dress. She plaited her hair and pulled on a kerchief, then went back down to find the bird still enjoying a pleasant interlude with Thumbelina.

"All right, come on, Jack." Beth held out her arm, and the parrot obligingly hopped on board. She started down the steps, hesitating for a moment as she wondered whether she needed a lantern, but

then decided the moon's glow was more than enough
to guide her.

Ransom woke gasping for breath and feeling tears
wet on his face. He didn't want to remember the
dream. He got up and stared out at the moonlit *nacht*
and decided to take a walk to cool his thoughts. He
quickly dressed, ran a hand through his ruffled hair,
and headed quietly downstairs. He took the back
staircase and went out the kitchen door so as not to
wake Aenti Ruth or her personal zoo.

He put his hands in his pockets and wandered
along the back road that led to the Mast residence,
not intending to do anything more than clear his
head. But then he heard the distinctive call of a
parrot and stopped to listen. "Ach, that bird," he
muttered, picking up his pace.

Just then, he saw Beth in front of him with Jack on
her shoulder. The moonlight touched her features,
framing them with a beautiful halo of silver. She
seemed almost ethereal as she approached. He felt
his heart thud hard in his chest as he softly said her
name. "Beth?"

She appeared startled, and he held out a hand to
her. "It's me," he said.

"Ach . . . Ransom, I—Jack came over when I was
sitting outside and I thought I'd bring him back
before Aenti Ruth found him missing."

"*Danki.* The bird is more trouble than he's worth."

He heard her soft giggle, and it struck him how
rarely he'd heard her laugh outright. He longed to
take her in his arms and tell her he loved her, but
his past opened like a gaping maw between them.

I cannot tell her the truth. . . . What would she think of me, of what I am? But maybe he could give her some of the truth . . . tell her something that would pass as the truth. He took a deep breath. "Beth, I–I need to tell you—when I was seventeen—the first summer at my grandfather's house . . ."

Memories surfaced, skipped through his mind like stones thrown over the water of a pond.

He saw Beth looking at him. "I was seventeen and I—She was—beautiful. More beautiful than any woman I'd ever seen, *Englisch* or Amish. I—we—I'd be exhausted from working all day, but I still saw her, didn't think. She was a bit older than me and it was—"

He paused and Beth finished for him. "True love."

He looked at her sadly and nodded. "Yeah—I guess."

He stepped closer to her. "I believe that you understand me, Beth. Will you tell me how you can understand?"

She shook her head and stepped back from him, while Jack fluttered restively.

Ransom didn't move, waiting for her to speak.

Beth was caught between the desire to tell him the truth and the certainty that lifting the veil between them would be a catastrophe. "I just understand," she murmured.

"Ah, little hare—I won't bite."

She looked at him; he was tall, strong, and now she knew somehow, very, very wounded. It was in her to want to take care of him, to want to save him and give him a good life. She didn't pause to wonder where *Gott* came into this giving, and she moved closer to him once more.

"I know . . . no biting," she murmured.

Then she was in his arms and felt as though spun sugar coated her body as he eased his mouth down the side of her neck and shoulder. His clever fingers pulled on her kerchief and the mass of her hair came loose from its plait and fell down about her back and shoulders.

She found herself eager to return his kisses and tentatively lifted her chin a bit. He groaned and moved his head, deepening the kiss until she had the strange sensation that they were both held in that moment by the moonlight and the magic between them. Some part of her weary soul came to temporary life.

"Ach, Ransom . . ."

He made a choked sound as he touched her hair and her back, and then they suddenly both froze in place as they heard a sharp female voice.

Chapter Twenty

"Hmmm!" Aenti Ruth called. "I *geh* out looking for a bird and find kissing by moonlight. Very interesting." She came closer and stamped her cane on the ground.

Ransom turned, his arms protective around Beth.

"It's not what it seems," he said gruffly.

"Oh, I know that." Aenti Ruth laughed. "Very few things in this world are what they seem to be."

"I mean," Ransom continued, "this wasn't a planned meeting."

"That I can believe as well. You both are out here to help an *auld* woman's favorite bird come home, and I dearly appreciate that. You have my word that no news of this, um, interlude will be repeated by either me or Jack." She held out her arm, and Jack easily came to perch on her shoulder. "I'll bid you two young people *gut nacht.*"

Ransom watched her turn and hobble off down the road, her gray hair illuminated by the moonlight.

He turned back to Beth. "I'll see you home."

She shook her head. "*Nee.* Viola might see . . . I mean, not that there's anything to see."

He laughed softly, then bent to swipe a quick kiss

across her cheek. "There's something, little hare. There's something . . ."

Friday morning dawned bright and clear, and Beth's stomach churned with expectation and excitement. She knew that the bishop himself was to bring a wagonful of people from their community to help lay the foundation for a new cabin for the pastor's wife and children.

Beth tied her apron neatly and skipped breakfast as she hurried to wash the dishes in the sink before the wagon came.

She couldn't help but overhear Viola complaining to Rose, but she knew that not even Viola would gainsay the expectations of Bishop Umble.

"It is, of course, right to help the *Englischers*," Viola mused loudly. "But a shame that we ourselves should lose the money from the pie stand this morning because of it."

It's better to give than to receive, Beth thought and told herself that she wasn't contradicting but merely stating a fact. She was spared any further thought on the matter when the sound of the wagon and horses rattled from the dirt road.

"Come, Rose, we will *geh* as well and see about this undertaking." Viola rose from the table and Beth turned and bit her lip. She wasn't sure if there'd be space in the wagon, and she sighed to think that her free time away for the day would be spent under strict supervision.

I'm becoming wanton, she thought. Swayed by Ransom's kisses. *It's strange—I haven't been kissed since my* fater *died. Why does Viola not show me affection as she does Rose? Of course, I'm not actually her daughter, not authentic, not real. I'm not real. I'm a freak and a glutton and*—Her negative diatribe was brought to an abrupt end by a knock at the door.

Beth turned from the sink to see Viola securing her bonnet and Bishop Umble at the screen door.

Viola hurried forward and opened the door. "Bishop, please come in. Rose and I were just preparing to join you."

"Well—" The bishop stroked his long white beard. "As to that, Widow Mast, I'm afraid we only have room left for Beth. The fellow who set this up with Ransom did so while he was with Beth after the fire. Did you not know? *Kumme* along, Beth. We mustn't dally. Rose can finish those dishes."

He held the screen door wide and Beth hurried to leave. "*Gutbye*, Viola and Rose."

She received no answer; nor had she expected one.

Ransom held the brake while the bishop handed Beth into the back with the other folks who were going. He glanced round at her and saw that she was comfortably settled next to Lucy, who was an excellent seamstress and was going along to see what clothes the women of the community might make to replace the ones that had been lost in the fire. Jeb and Abel were also there, as well as several other expert carpenters and women bearing food for everyone.

Bishop Umble was inclined to be talkative and held Ransom's attention until they arrived at the site of the fire. Strangely, Ransom saw Ryan Mason step from beneath the tall pines and reach up to shake hands with the bishop and the wagon's other occupants.

Ransom jumped down and tied off the horses. He moved, intending to swing Beth over the side of the wagon, and was annoyed when Ryan reached her first. But he was quick to note that Beth seemed little interested in attentions from the *Englischer*. She began to whisper, then giggle with Lucy as they looked his way.

Ransom felt himself flush and cursed softly under his breath. *What am I? In school still, that the attentions of a girl can make me blush?* But he had to admit that Beth was no ordinary *maedel*. . . .

"Ach, Beth," Lucy whispered with matronly certainty. "Ransom is more than smitten with you. Did you see his face when that Ryan lifted you down?"

"*Nee*," Beth protested, but Lucy grabbed her hand and pulled her to the side by some sprawling mountain laurel.

"What are you not telling me?" Lucy demanded with a smile. "Ach, he's kissed you."

"*Nee*," Beth whispered feebly, then couldn't contain her smile at the obvious untruth.

"How many times? Ach, if he kisses anything like Jeb . . ."

"Ahem!" Bishop Umble interrupted them with a twinkle in his bright blue eyes. "Sorry to barge in, but this is Mrs. Lott. Her husband was the pastor who passed on from this world to the next. She's thinking of going back to Williamsport—she and her children lost all their things in the fire—but I told her that I'd like her to stay on a bit until the new cabins are built. She'll stay with Martha and myself. I thought you and the other women might be able to help her out with some clothing for her and the *kinner*."

Beth recognized the woman as the harried lady who had bought her first pies. *No wonder she looks like she's struggling—to lose her husband like that—so young.*

Beth reached out a hand to the older woman, as did Lucy. Mrs. Lott gave them a wan smile.

"Please call me Olivia. And the children are Sienna, April, and May. They've been all out of sorts since their father . . . Well, since the fire."

Beth saw the blond-haired woman's blue eyes swim with tears, which she hastily swiped away; it was as if she were tired of crying.

"Why don't I take the children for some breakfast while you *geh* into the barn nearby and let Beth take some measurements?" Lucy suggested with a smile.

Beth saw that Olivia looked askance at their Amish dresses and had to smile. "I can sew most anything, Mrs.—er, Olivia. How do some shorts and nice blouses sound?"

"Wonderful. Thank you."

Beth nodded and led Olivia back to the barn, trying to forget about the day in the rain, when she and Ransom had kissed inside it.

"Are you married?"

Beth flushed at the question, almost as if her thoughts about Ransom had revealed themselves to the world. "Uh . . . *nee*. . . ." she stammered.

"Oh, I'm sorry for asking. It's strange, but when you're a—widow—it seems as if every other woman on the planet has someone in her life."

"You must miss your husband very much. I–I'm so sorry."

Olivia swiped at her eyes once more as they reached the barn and slid the door open. "I keep thinking it might just be a bad dream; that I'll wake up and everything will be the same. But I know that's not going to happen."

Beth sought for something to say as she drew her tape measure from her apron pocket.

"I—my *fater* died . . ." The words sounded small and insignificant in comparison to Olivia's grief, and Beth was surprised she had uttered them.

"Did you hate God for a while?" the *Englischwoman* asked ruefully.

Beth stood stock still as the question resonated throughout her soul. "I—" *Did I? Do I?* "I—have been angry with Him—" It was a truth that nearly took her breath away.

Olivia waved a hand tiredly. "Please forget I asked. I know your Amish faith probably doesn't dwell on negative things like that."

"*Nee*, oh no, I'd like to know, please. Did you— hate Him for a while?"

"I still do," Olivia admitted quietly. "Jim was a good man, and so young. He was a good father, husband, and pastor. I don't understand . . . when there are so many . . . evil men . . ." She broke off and straightened her back with obvious resolution. "I'm truly sorry." She extended her arms. "Please take your measurements."

Beth bit her lip as she stretched out the yellow tape. "My *daed* was a good man too. I—it wasn't his fault that he died. . . ." *It was mine. Mine. Mine* . . . She sighed deeply at the treacherous thoughts. "I suppose being *gut* or bad has nothing to do with dying."

Olivia leaned forward and suddenly held her in a tight embrace. "It's so strange that you say that . . . it was the name of the last sermon Jim preached." She pulled back to stare into Beth's eyes. "I haven't thought of it, what with everything that's been going on. But . . . he said that God is in charge of the time you die . . . that he knows the day you were born . . . the number of hairs on your head . . . the number of tears you shed. . . ." She sobbed the last words through a smile that caused Beth's heart to skip a beat. "Thank you, Beth. Thank you for helping me remember. It's a great comfort; like I've got some equilibrium back."

Beth nodded, her own eyes full of tears, and whispered with tenderness, "Praise *Gott*. You're welcome."

Chapter Twenty-One

Ransom had a sudden idea as he watched fellow Amish men arrive with wagons full of lumber to frame out the cabins. He turned and sought out the bishop in the small crowd, noting that Beth was nowhere to be seen.

"Ach, Ransom, looking for Beth?"

Ransom frowned into the discerning blue eyes of Bishop Umble and automatically shook his head. "*Nee* . . . I was . . . um . . . looking for you actually."

"Well, here I am."

"Right. I was thinking that, instead of renting these cabins out to the *Englisch* like we usually do. . . . We should offer them as cabins of rest, a place where folks could *kumme* for a donation or for free, just to heal from the world. . . ." Ransom trailed off, unsure whether his idea was too far-fetched, but Bishop Umble was smiling.

"The Cabins of Rest on Ice Mountain. I think we could advertise and it could be a great spring-through-autumn retreat for folks!" The bishop clapped him heartily on the shoulder. "Excellent idea, *sohn*."

Ransom nodded, awash with the leader's affirmation. It felt *gut*, but then he remembered the past with a swamping dread. The bishop's hand tightened on Ransom's shoulder and the *auld* man leaned close. "Do you understand grace, Ransom King?"

He said the first thing that came into his head. "People don't talk like that. . . ."

Bishop Umble smiled. "*Nee*, I suppose not, but they want to . . . they want to ask those kinds of questions, but evil has a way of trying to silence grace."

"I guess the voice of . . . grace . . . has been pretty silent in my life."

"Then let it in, *buwe*. Give it as much of a chance as you've given the darkness that holds you."

Ransom swallowed as the bishop walked away. The *auld* leader stirred his heart and made him feel as if someone had touched his very soul. He looked around instinctively for Beth, wanting to share the idea with her.

She and Mrs. Lott were walking toward him, and he swiped at his eyes as they approached.

Beth noticed that Ransom's dark eyes seemed to glimmer in the sunshine and she smiled in greeting, longing to tell him of what Olivia had said to her in the barn, but she noticed a sketchbook under his arm. "What's that?" she asked curiously.

"Ach, some furniture sketches of mine. I thought the family might like to choose some pieces and different woods—Daed's got quite a supply back at the shop and I've ordered some other wood types in."

Beth smiled faintly. "It's funny, I've lived among the Amish all my life and should know wood types,

I suppose." She wrinkled her nose. "But all I can think of are cherry, walnut, and pine."

"Oh, me too," Olivia Lott said tremulously. "My grandfather was a carpenter, but I know very little about his work other than remembering sitting on his workshop steps and watching him use all these fascinating tools. He made me a dollhouse that had a spiral staircase. . . . I still had it up until the fire. The children played with it. . . ." Her kind face and blue eyes looked wan but resolute. "Still, God had something good in mind when he brought you to us."

Beth impulsively reached out and touched her arm. "Ach, *jah*, and you to us."

Ransom smiled at the pair of women. "Perhaps, Mrs. Lott, you might care to look through our sketchbook and pick out some furniture. My family and I would be glad to make it for you. . . . It may take some time, but I plan to hire a few more men at the shop, so it shouldn't be too long."

Olivia's eyes filled with tears and she gladly bent over the book Ransom held out. It made him feel righteous for once, for a brief moment. But then he wondered if he hid in his work, lost himself somewhere in all the scrollwork and fancy trimmings. . . . *Do I know what grace is* . . . He straightened his back and tried to concentrate on showing the drawings to Mrs. Lott. He admitted to himself that he felt shy almost, while Beth stood there quietly listening, but it also felt *gut*.

He cleared his throat. "Among the hardwoods

you can choose from, we have northern red oak, quarter-sawn white oak, cherry, maple, beech, elm, mahogany, walnut, hickory, cedar, and pine."

"Oh my," Beth murmured. "How can she choose? They all sound beautiful."

"*Danki.*" Ransom smiled at her. "Well, let me describe some of the woods when they're finished and maybe we can write down what pieces of furniture you want in each wood."

Olivia swallowed visibly and shook her head slowly. "You're both so kind, but I–I have no money to pay for fine furnishings. I'm really limited . . ."

"But *Gott* is not limited," Ransom said easily. "And besides, you'll be helping me by letting me keep some furniture on display to raise interest in our expanding furniture business. If my *daed* was here, he would thank you too. He's at home today . . . but let's *geh* sit in the shade and I'll show you what I've got."

They made their way to a copse of maple trees and sat down on the grass. Ransom took out a pencil nub and a clean sheet of paper. "Now, cherry is nice. It has a light, reddish-brown color that will darken with exposure to the sun. It might be really *gut* for a dining-room table and chairs. Although maple is lovely too. It's significantly harder than oak and is growing in popularity because of its beauty."

Ransom glanced at Beth while Olivia thought, and he imagined what it might be like to build furniture for Beth—for a home of their own. *I am losing my mind . . . and she deserves so much more. . . .*

"Oh, Mr. King," Olivia exclaimed. "Can I just leave

it to you and your family to choose what is right? We'd be so glad of anything you create."

Ransom nodded and remembered to smile, though his mind was far away, lost in an image of golden-haired children sitting around a walnut-stained table while Beth sat opposite him and they all quieted for grace . . .

Beth savored the movements of Ransom's lean hands as he paged through the drawings for Olivia and her to inspect. She realized the time spent with his grandfather had opened a well of creativity in Ransom that shone in each bold sketch. She watched him as he explained each piece of furniture and the wood he might choose, and she knew that he had a gifted mind for such things. Then she remembered what it was like to be held by his capable hands and couldn't resist the shiver of delight that ran down her back. Was this what it was to love someone? she wondered, finding that even the cadence of his voice gave her pleasure. She clenched her hands in her lap and tasted the secret thought that Ransom could be hers . . . could love her back . . . if only . . .

The following week, at the site of the cabins, timber was being delivered from the Kings' woodshop, and the pungent smell of fresh-cut pine and maple hung heavy in the air. "I'm glad you thought of making these cabins a place of rest for both Amish and *Englisch* alike, Ransom," Bishop Umble said heartily, and Ransom tried to drink in the compliment. as he and the spiritual leader walked about the worksite.

"It's a pleasure and a privilege to help," Ransom returned. "But there is one thing . . ."

"You name it."

Ransom shrugged. "You seem to carry the burdens of the past so lightly on your shoulders. I mean, dealing with this fire and the role of leadership. And I'm sure there have been other things that you and your family have had to face in the past. I don't know . . . I just wondered if there is some secret to it."

Bishop Umble smiled. "It's not a secret surely, but perhaps not something you've considered before. We don't tell ourselves enough of *Gott's* Truth. . . . In any case, for us humans, time and the past seem immutable—unable to be changed."

"But that's the truth, right?" Ransom asked.

"Well, as humans on this earth, we're forced to think in linear time. We can't go back, become young again, or undo something that has wounded us in the past. But to *Gott*, time is not immutable. He lives for and in all time. He holds our lives in His Hands and He is capable of going back in our pasts and bringing goodness or wisdom or, especially, truth from the things we've experienced into today."

"Whew!" Ransom tipped back his hat on his brow. "That sounds complicated!"

"Maybe this sounds less difficult—we have to learn to forgive ourselves for our pasts as *Gott* forgives."

"No," Ransom answered soberly. "That sounds much more difficult."

Bishop Umble paused in his walking and turned to face him. "Is there something, Ransom, that you need to forgive yourself for?"

"I wouldn't know where to begin," he said softly.

The bishop shot him an encouraging nod. "I didn't

say it was easy—in fact, I think it's easier to forgive
others sometimes because we feel they deserve it.
But ourselves . . . no, we don't deserve forgiveness
in our own eyes."

Ransom nodded and exhaled, but he couldn't do
what Bishop Umble was talking about. In fact, he was
sure the spiritual leader wouldn't even want to be
talking to him if he knew everything . . . if he knew
about them . . .

As she peered from her small loft window, Beth
watched Bishop and Martha Umble walk away from
the cabin. She had heard someone knock earlier and
had hastened to the loft ladder to *geh* and answer the
door, but Viola had been up—oddly enough. Then
Beth had listened shamelessly and caught various
words that made her heart sing.

It seemed that the *gut* spiritual leader of Ice
Mountain had suggested that Viola and Rose stay at
home and sew the clothes for the Lott family while
Beth be allowed to *kumme* and *geh* from the worksite.

"Because you know what a treasure she is," Martha
Umble had said in rather wry tones.

And Viola had hastily murmured some agreement.

Beth had thanked *Gott* as she retreated from the
top of the ladder, thrilled that she would surely see
Ransom every day.

Aenti Ruth had asked Ransom if she might come
along, and that meant, of course, that the zoo was
coming too. But Ransom had somehow become used

to the noise and thought the little Lott *kinner* might enjoy playing with the animals.

Second John had filled out nicely, and his odd-colored fur had taken on a distinctive, healthy sheen. Ransom helped Aenti Ruth down from the wagon and then proceeded to unload Petunia and Pig. Jack flew companionably along beside the others.

"How big is each cabin going to be, Ransom?" Aenti Ruth asked imperiously as a worker brushed past her and nearly tripped on her cane. He murmured a quick apology and hurried back to his task, and Aenti Ruth harrumphed and adjusted her bonnet.

"The cabin will be big enough for the three Lott children," Ransom replied.

"Ach, *jah*," Aenti Ruth said, and for the first time Ransom noticed a softening in her tone. "*Kinner*," Ruth continued. "It has always been my regret that Isaiah and I never had any children."

"I don't remember Uncle Isaiah all that well," Ransom said.

Aenti Ruth nodded. "He was killed when we had been married only ten years." She continued in a soft, almost wistful tone, "He had a *gut* laugh."

Ransom nodded, unsure of what to say.

Aenti Ruth cleared her throat. "Ransom, let's go look at the space for the kitchen cabinets."

Just then, one of the Lott children came around the corner of the roughed-out cabin, riding on Petunia's back. The pig squealed happily, and the little girl laughed with glee.

Ransom thought it a cute sight and smiled himself, until Petunia made a beeline straight for Aenti Ruth. Despite Ransom's hold, Aenti Ruth was bowled over in a pile of skirts, old-fashioned shoes, and pig squeals.

"Oh dear!"

Ransom heard the feminine cry of distress above the surrounding noise. "Aenti Ruth!" he called, "are you alright?"

Petunia had stopped, and now stood penitently by while Ransom tried to help Aenti Ruth sit up. The little Lott girl had run off.

Aenti Ruth sat up, but Ransom noticed immediately that she reached to rub her right ankle. He realized she was stiff-lipped with pain, and quickly gathered her up in his arms. He called for Jeb to bring the wagon so they might *geh* to Sarah's cabin. But he wondered worriedly if the wagon ride would be too rough.

"The wagon will be fine, Ransom," Aenti Ruth said, making up his mind for him. "I'm not going anywhere without my animals. And besides, dear Petunia feels guilty. And she shouldn't."

Ransom supposed he could only agree.

Chapter Twenty-Two

Bishop Umble seemed to have had a great effect on Viola, and Beth was told that she would be able to *geh* and help at the cabins more often than not—though she still had to keep up with her chores at home. But Beth didn't mind that.

Today, she and Lucy arrived at the worksite in Lucy's buggy just as Ransom was loading the last animal into the wagon. Beth jumped down and hurried over to the side of the wagon to look at Aenti Ruth's pale face.

"Oh my! Ransom, what happened? Is there anything I can do to help?"

"*Nee*, I'm going to take her to Sarah's."

"Let the girl ride back here, Ransom. It will be a comfort to me," Aenti Ruth muttered.

Beth jumped into the wagon without preamble or waiting for Ransom's approval. The ride to Sarah's seemed overly long, and Beth tried to steady the awkward ankle while silently praying for Aenti Ruth. Fortunately, the healer was home, hanging out wash to dry. Beth watched as Ransom lifted his aunt with tender hands and carried her through the cabin door.

Sarah directed them to the bed in the room behind the busy kitchen, where she took off Aenti Ruth's shoe while Beth held the *auld* lady's hand. Ransom paced with visible anxiety while Jack clung to his shoulder.

"Sprained. Badly," Sarah pronounced after a long moment. "Ransom, if you'll hold your *aenti*'s foot steady, I'll put some strapping on it."

Beth bit her own lip as she felt Aenti Ruth's aged hand tighten against hers while Sarah finished stabilizing the injured foot. But Sarah worked quickly and soon had Aenti Ruth relaxing against the plump feather pillows with some tea she brewed for pain.

"She can rest here today, Ransom. And then I want her to put no weight on her foot for at least a week."

"We'll have to tie her down," Ransom quipped, but Beth could tell that he was glad the diagnosis wasn't more serious for his *aenti*.

Beth realized that she was able to read his emotions to some extent, and the feeling of insight was heady.

But she was surprised when they left Sarah's *haus* and he took her hand, almost absently. *Perhaps he'll kiss me again.* . . . The thought made her shiver with delight. But then she noticed that his expression was sober and distant, and she waited to hear what he'd say.

"Beth . . ." Ransom found himself at a loss for words. Then he closed his eyes for a moment and turned to face her.

"I'm sure Ruth will be well. She's a strong woman," Beth hastened to assure him.

"She is strong, that's true. But . . . that's not it. I—Let's walk in the woods for a bit, can we?"

"Of course," she agreed, her pretty face flushed.

He knew instinctively that she wanted to be kissed, and he longed for the touch of her soft mouth as well. But he knew he wanted to try to tell her . . . something . . . anything.

"Please don't worry so much, Ransom."

He looked at her. "Actually, I was thinking about the last time I was trying to help someone who was in great pain. . . ."

"When was that?" Beth asked quietly.

Ransom shoved his hands in his pockets and turned to stare out at the trees. "When the girl I—Barbara . . . She died," he said baldly, then bent his head. *They died . . . they died . . .*

"Your—the *maedel*—your true love died?"

"*Jah* . . . but she wasn't . . ."

"She—she was ill?"

"*Nee*, it was—it was what they called an accident, but it wasn't. It was my doing, my fault." He looked at her then, expecting to see the horror in her blue eyes, but instead he encountered grief to match his own. . . .

Beth stared up into his dark eyes, wanting to be present, to say something of comfort to him, but she had been catapulted into her own waking *nachtmare*. She felt her heart begin to pound in her ears and knew once more the swamping guilt and pain. . . .

She wet her lips and swallowed hard, longing to run, but then, suddenly, she was in his arms and he was kissing her with deft, hard strokes, as if he wanted to drive something from her mind . . . *from his mind . . .*

She kissed him in return as she had never done before. She put her hands against his chest and felt the muscled flesh beneath the blue of his shirt. Her fingers convulsed against this hidden pleasure and she heard him groan deep in his throat. She had a strange sense of connection within her own body. She felt as if she was spinning at each touch of his lips and wanted the moment to go on forever. . . .

He broke away from her with all the suddenness of a dousing in icy creek water and she stepped back, feeling herself gasp for breath.

"I'm sorry, little hare," he muttered. "But we're no more than twenty feet from the main trail—anyone could see."

She nodded in understanding. *Of course he wouldn't want anyone to see . . . not stolen kisses with the likes of me . . . but oh, I can live on these experiences for the rest of my life. . . .*

"Beth?" His questioning tone brought her out of her own musings and she looked up at him to find his cheeks ruddy with color and his dark eyes narrowed, as if he were in pain of some sort.

She reached out automatically to touch his arm and heard his sharp, indrawn breath.

"Ach, Beth," he said. "How I wish you could understand, that you could know—"

Then tell me, she thought, but she didn't speak aloud, not when she herself was so reluctant to let him see what hid in her own heart. . . .

* * *

He shouldn't have kissed her. . . . The thought ran around in his head, intermixed with the unadulterated pleasure he'd felt touching his mouth to hers. It was becoming an indulgent habit, and he knew he had no right to tell her that he loved her and that he wanted . . . *What do I want? To court her? To make love to her? And then what?*

He let his mind drift dangerously close to the memory of what had happened in the past, and then he was lost. . . . He was once again seventeen, hearing Barbara's screams. The smell of smoke and blood hovered in the air, choking him. Ransom clawed desperately at the car door, but he was unable to open the mangled frame. Once more, he heard Barbara scream his name, but there was nothing he could do to save her—to save them. . . .

Chapter Twenty-Three

The next evening, Beth lathered barbeque sauce on the baked meatloaf, then set it back into the oven. The potatoes were ready to mash and she drained them, then poured them back into the blue bowl with the chip on its edge. She added a stick of butter and salt and just a touch of cream, then hurried to use the potato masher to create a smooth and fluffy mass. She had lemon sponge cake for afters . . . but she knew she would only be able to peck at her food while in the presence of Viola and Rose. She'd eat the remainder of the potatoes in private later on that night. . . .

At supper, the talk was mostly of Viola's birthday, which was coming up in a few days. Rose had cornered Beth in the pantry and told her that she was going to see Ransom later that evening to ask him about crafting a spice box for Viola. Beth had stared at her stepsister. "A spice box? For the kitchen? But Viola never cooks—I cook."

This was a dawning realization for Beth as she spoke the truth in a way she normally didn't.

"Of course you make a dish here and there," Rose said testily.

"I cook." Beth savored the rush of freedom that came with the simple words. *I cook*, she thought. The words were almost better than fresh strawberry jam on a spoon. . . .

Ransom watched Abel's movements out of the corner of his eye. The workshop normally hummed with the sounds of pneumatic drills and hammering, but it was nearly silent now, as if his little *bruder* carried as much on his mind as Ransom did himself.

"How's the girl . . . situation, Abel?"

The *buwe* shrugged. "We broke up."

Ransom paused in running the lathe down a piece of cherrywood. "I'm sorry, Abel. What happened?"

"Nuthin' . . . she decided she preferred an *Englischer*, that's all."

"Yeah, but that hurts, I bet, just the same." Ransom cleared his throat. "Did you . . . Did she . . ."

Abel met his gaze with a hint of a smile playing about his lips. "*Nee*, big *bruder*. We didn't . . . but someday . . . with the right *maedel* . . ."

Ransom nodded. "That makes you a wiser young man than I was, Abel; much wiser."

"You had an *Englisch* girlfriend?"

Ransom turned back to the cherrywood. "Never mind." He knew his voice was gruff, but he had no desire to visit the dark corners of his mind yet again. He sighed aloud, then forced himself to concentrate on the variations in the color of the wood.

A bit later, Ransom looked up from lathing a piece

of maple and listened to the sound of a buggy and a horse in the cool evening air. He looked up expectantly, hoping it would be Beth. He went out into the gloaming and recognized Rose alone in the buggy.

Great . . . He went around with a sigh and reached up a hand to help her down.

"Ach, Ransom . . . I'm so glad to catch you alone. . . ."

"Catch" being the operative word here, he thought.

"Why is that?" *And where's Beth . . . ?*

"Why, my mother's birthday, of course. I was hoping you'd have a spice box or perhaps a keepsake box already made in the shop that I could purchase. Her birthday's this week."

"Sure," he said politely. "If you'll stay here, I'll *geh* and look."

"*Ach,* no, I'm afraid of bats."

"Bats?"

"*Jah.* Besides, won't it be fun to be alone in the workshop?"

Nee . . .

"Sure," he said again. "Where's Beth?" he asked casually.

Rose simpered. "Oh, home, doing something or other. You know how much she likes the housework."

"Right."

He led her into the dusky workshop and turned up another lantern. They had a supply of items that were ready for sale in a room at the back, but he had no intention of getting caught with Rose Mast alone in a secluded spot. He invited her to sit down at the workbench, then hurried to the back and grabbed up a spice box. It was a simple thing, really—more like a rack. But it was pretty, with small, patterned scrolls on the front. It was just right for a birthday present.

When he came back, he found Rose poring over his sketchbook. "Ransom! I didn't realize you were so talented," she said.

Uh-huh, he thought.

He showed her the box.

"How much will that be?" she asked. "It's beautiful."

He waved a hand in dismissal. "Just take it and wish Viola well."

"All right," she said, seeming at a loss for how else she might stretch out the moment. He opened the door of the woodshop and was prepared to lead her back outside.

"Oh my!" she said. "I nearly forgot. I brought flowers for your Aenti Ruth. May I see her?"

"Well, you know, she's bound to be tired."

"It'll only take a minute."

Ransom sighed and led her to the porch after she retrieved the flowers from the buggy.

Petunia had taken to guarding Aenti Ruth since the accident and truly seemed a penitent pig. However, Ransom could tell right away that Petunia, for whatever reason, had taken a distinct dislike to Rose. The pig made a grunting sound low in her throat, and Rose jumped back and grabbed Ransom's arm.

"Ransom!" Ruth said irritably from the couch where she was lying. "What is going on? I'm trying to sleep."

"Here's Rose Mast, Aenti Ruth. She brought you some flowers."

"Bah!" Aenti Ruth said. "What good are flowers to a sprained ankle? Tell the twit to go home!"

Ransom turned to Rose. "Aenti Ruth is not herself.

Maybe it would be better if you came back another day." But Rose flounced past him and Petunia to go to Aenti Ruth's side.

"Oh, Frau Mast. I'm sure you would love the flowers. Beth—I mean, um, I–I picked them just this evening."

Ransom rolled his eyes.

"That's right," Aenti Ruth said. "Beth picked them, I have no doubt. Now please, go on home."

As if to emphasize the point, Second John jumped down from the chair and started growling in his puppy way. He bared his little canines and Rose once more seemed frightened. Soon, each of the animals was adding to the sounds in the room. Pig was wheeking, Jack flew around sporadically, and Matthew, Mark, and Luke started to circle threateningly.

Rose fled, dropping the flowers, dashing past Ransom and out into the night.

"Good riddance to bad rubbish," Aenti Ruth groaned.

Ransom had to agree. He bent and picked up the flowers gently from the floor and walked to offer them to Aenti Ruth. "I think these flowers were actually from Beth. Would you cherish them more if you knew they were from her?"

Aenti Ruth blinked pain-filled eyes at him and smiled. "The question is, *buwe*, would you cherish them more?"

Beth smiled as she washed the dishes in the evening twilight and reflected on the trust and acceptance the Lott children seemed to place in Ransom. He would make a wonderful father, she thought. *But with some other girl, maybe . . . Barbara . . . someone like Barbara . . .* Then she slowed her thoughts, and some part of her stood up a little straighter. *But he's kissing me, sharing his work with me, playing with the children with me . . .* She thought back to a recent afternoon at the worksite. Beth had realized that the children were running wild while their* mamm *was involved with plans for the cabin. Beth decided to teach the* kinner *a game she'd liked to play herself when she was little.

"Sienna, April, May, kumme*! I will show you a fun way to spend the afternoon."

She had led them to a spot that had been untouched by the fire and sat down on the grass beneath a comforting maple tree. "Let's play restaurant," she'd said with a smile.

"We need to have different people in the restaurant. When you go to a restaurant for real, who is in the restaurant?"

Sienna raised her hand. "The customers!"

"Right," Beth had replied. "So, we need a customer . . . who else is there?"

"The cook!" Sienna replied again.

"And there's one more person in the restaurant . . ."

May took her thumb out of her mouth and smiled. "The waiter!"

"Great!" Beth had laughed at the imaginary fun. "All right, so who wants to be who in our restaurant?"

"I want to be the waiter," Sienna said.

"I want to be the cook," April said.

But May pouted. "I wanted to be the cook."

"All right, we'll have two cooks," Beth soothed, heading off an argument. "And I'll be the customer."

Just then, a male voice joined the conversation, and Beth looked up to see Ransom standing above them.

"Can I be a customer too?" he asked.

"Sure." *Beth smiled, pleased he was willing to play with the children.*

Ransom sat down next to her.

"Pretend you're married," *Sienna suggested brightly.*

Beth couldn't help the flush that she knew stained her cheeks, and it surely didn't help matters when Ransom gave her a wolfish grin.

"Okay," *Beth said, taking a breath.* "Herr, er, King and I are the customers. So, we give our order to the waiter and the cooks go off and cook!"

"We need 'gredients for our recipes," *April cried.*

"What are we going to use for ingredients? We don't have a refrigerator out here," *Sienna said logically.*

"Well, we pretend. For example . . ." *Beth had pulled a leaf from the ground.* "You can use a large leaf as a plate."

Beth glanced sideways at Ransom, and he hastily grabbed some grass between his fingers. "And grass can be your salad!"

"And sticks can be forks!" *Sienna smiled, passing one to Ransom.*

The game had gone on for a gut *twenty minutes—long enough for Beth to wish that she might become Frau King one day. . . .*

Now she tested the thoughts against her normal insecurities and found that the truths could hold their own weight. It was like a candle in the snow, and she held the idea close to her heart.

Later that evening, Ransom bent over the worktable in the back of the woodshop, showing his *fater* the sketch choices Mrs. Lott had picked out.

"The children's furniture would look *gut* in

hickory sapwood. Just right for little girls, with its bright white, and it's stronger than oak to stand up to quite a few years of wear and tear," his *fater* mused, tracing a finger across the page. "As a matter of fact, it might be nice to start on a few of these for when the *grandkinner* come about." His *fater* nudged him gently with a smile.

Ransom nudged him back. "You've got to be talking about Jeb and Lucy . . . right?"

"I heard from your *mamm* that Beth Mast was over here the other day. . . ."

"Daed." Ransom sighed.

"Go on now, *sohn*. I'm only teasing."

"I know." Ransom smiled, but then sobered as something came to his mind. "Hey, Daed . . . can you tell me how Beth's *fater* died?"

"Ach, that's a sad telling, *sohn*." His *fater* considered. "But I'll tell you just the same. Chet Mast was a *gut* friend, and at times, I miss him sorely. But . . . he was killed in a buggy accident one afternoon on the way home from Coudersport."

"I knew that." Ransom nodded. "But was there anything—strange about what happened?"

"Strange?"

"Ach, I don't know what I mean. . . . It's just that Beth appears so pale and almost frozen by terror when I've chanced to mention her *fater*."

"Well, you know, there was one thing strange, now that I think of it. Beth herself couldn't be found after the accident. Some of the men even started to search for her. Chet had taken her along to enjoy the ride."

"Where was she?"

"In a cornfield."

"Near the accident site?"

"*Nee*, nearly a mile away. It's a wonder we found the child. She was silent for days, even through the funeral. Then she slowly seemed to come back to herself."

Ransom thought hard and determined to gently ask Beth about that day. *Though what right do I have to pry into the past? I certainly couldn't bear anyone looking into mine. . . . Still, she is my friend . . . my friend with kisses . . . who I love.*

The following day, Beth was tired after spending most of the hot afternoon at the worksite playing with the *kinner*, but she was also grateful for time next to Ransom on the ride home.

"I had fun with you and the girls today," she said with a smile.

He gave her an absentminded nod. "Me too."

She was silent for a few minutes, sensing he was deep in thought. "Is everything all right, Ransom?"

"Hmmm? *Jah*—I—was just thinking of a conversation I had with Bishop Umble, and it kind of weighs on me."

"What did you talk about?"

"The past." He half-turned to look at her. "How we have to forgive ourselves for the past."

Beth felt overwhelming desolation. As if that were possible, she thought with sudden and deep pain. She turned to look out at the cornfields, growing high with the summer sun. She remembered how their leaves had felt—cool and stiff against her skin.

And had to drag her mind back to the present when she realized Ransom was speaking.

"Beth?"

"*Jah*—I'm sorry."

"Don't be sorry. I was just asking about the day your *daed* died . . . My *fater* told me you were missing for part of that day. . . . Do you remember where you were?"

"In a cornfield," she said slowly. Then something in her rebelled and screamed that he had no right to question her about that day. "I don't want to talk about it."

She saw him nod, but he went on, almost musing. "I thought you might have seen the accident or—"

"I said that I don't want to talk about it," she shrilled, then leaped down from the slow-moving wagon and just barely cleared the wheel.

Ransom pulled back on the reins and Benny protested with a loud noise. Beth covered her ears and ran into the Loftus' cornfield without looking back.

Chapter Twenty-Four

Ransom pulled Benny off to the side of the dirt road, then jumped down and dove into the high corn, following Beth's path.

"Beth! Beth, stop!"

But she kept going and he had to run, diving through the stalks. He finally caught up with her and nearly fell over her huddled form on the ground in front of him.

"Beth?" He gentled his voice, as if he were speaking to some wild fawn he'd found, and sank down beside her. "Beth? Honey . . . what is it?"

She spoke no words but let out a low, keening wail, her small mouth open and her eyes closed. He recognized her abject misery and it tore at his heart. He tried to put his arms around her, but she jerked away from him. He could only kneel beside her, listening to her cry.

This lasted for several long minutes until, finally, she quieted and was still, her head bent low. He waited, saying nothing, but praying hard inside for her, praying that he would have the wisdom to know what to do for her.

He took a deep breath. "Aenti Ruth says you know

a powerful secret." He wanted to kick himself, but nothing else had come to mind except to speak of the commonplace things in their lives.

"Do you know a secret, little hare?"

To his immense relief, she nodded slowly, still not opening her eyes.

"Yeah, I know one too. . . . Our secrets make us kindred spirits. Did you know that, Beth? We have companionship in our suffering and companionship with Derr Herr—that's something pretty special, don't you think?"

He listened to her breathing slow as she shuddered, then swiped her hands across her runny nose. He gently reached out two fingers and touched her sleeve, a whisper of a touch; she opened her eyes. She looked around, seeming to take in her surroundings for the first time. Then she looked at him, her eyes wide open. He risked gathering her to him and she yielded. He leaned over and picked her up as he got to his feet.

"Ach, Ransom," she said in a choked whisper, and he cuddled her close, his own heartbeat finally slowing to normal as he strode back through the corn with her in his arms.

Later that night, in her bed, Beth thought about the moments in the cornfield. She wasn't sure, but she thought she owed Ransom an apology. It had all happened so fast . . . just like that day. She thought about what she had done then, when she was younger, and knew she hadn't cried. Not then. Just running, running, free . . .

She sighed aloud and reached down beside her to

touch Thumbelina, who purred contentedly at her presence. "Well," she whispered to the cat, "I might as well do something productive and start on the sewing for the *dollhaus*."

Ransom had shared with her that he and his *fater* had framed out a *dollhaus* to give to Olivia Lott. "A dollhouse!" she'd cried happily. "For Mrs. Lott. You remembered what she said about her grandfather's dollhouse being burned in the fire. . . . How kind you are, Ransom."

"*Danki*, Beth. The *haus* is made of pine."

"I can almost smell it. Pine smells so like Christmas!"

He'd nodded. "And it has a spiral staircase planned."

"You remembered she said it had a spiral staircase . . . you really listened."

"Thank you," he'd said softly. "I was hoping you could give me advice on colors for the rooms, and perhaps sew little cushions or rugs, and curtains for the windows. I want the window frames to *geh* up and down. . . . Anyway, I hope we can work on this together, and that it might be a special gift we leave in the cabin for her and the *kinner*."

Beth had caught his hand and given it an impulsive squeeze. "*Danki*, Ransom. I'd love to build it with you."

Now she stayed up late, carefully crafting tiny pillows and miniature quilts from her sewing scrap bag. She also braided four miniature rugs and sewed each one together. Beth realized that it might be fun to teach the Lott girls how to do some sewing and decided to take her sewing kit with her the next time she went to the worksite.

Finally, she grew tired and drifted off, holding

Thumbelina close, as if he might ward off any bad dreams.

Talking with Aenti Ruth while she was taking Sarah's herbal pain medicine was interesting, to say the least. So far that early morning, Ransom had been directed to remove an imaginary beaver from the tabletop and pull an elephant from his *aenti*'s old-fashioned shoe. But then she settled down, and he was able to share the chair by the couch with Petunia. "So, what do you think of Beth's secret?" she asked in a slurred voice.

"I don't know it, or at least not all of it," he returned quietly.

Aenti Ruth stretched to pat his knee. "She'll tell you when she's *gut* and ready. 'Tell the truth in love'— she needs to feel your love, Ransom . . . and get that *narrisch* squirrel off the table; it'll scare Jack."

Ransom didn't bother to deny what his *aenti* was saying—chances were the *auld* lady wouldn't remember saying it anyway. But she was right; he knew that deep inside, even as he removed the imaginary squirrel from the tabletop.

Chapter Twenty-Five

Beth beat the egg whites until her arm and shoulder were stiff, but finally, they began to form stiff little peaks. She added cream of tartar and vanilla and almond extract, as well as the dry ingredients, then poured the lot into a tube pan. She would make the frothy, boiled icing later. It was Viola's favorite cake and today was her birthday. Beth wanted to surprise her with it after supper that evening.

Next, she concentrated on getting the pies ready to take with her to share at the worksite; then she went to look out the window at the oncoming dawn. She turned hastily when she heard a soft knock at the back screen door. Her heart began to thump in her chest as she realized it was Ransom.

She went to open the door, unsure of how she should behave after the incident yesterday, but then he came in and smiled at her and everything felt normal again.

"Ransom, I'm sorry about yesterday. I–I can't really explain what happened, but I was scared. I appreciate your help and kindness." She knew she sounded rather stiff, but she couldn't let him know anything else.

He bent down and put his arms around her. She didn't pull away, yet at the same time she wasn't sure of herself with him. "It was my—honor to be with you in those moments, little hare. And no, I don't understand completely, but I think *Gott* is moving in our lives, and that is powerful."

She hadn't thought about it like that, but a sudden image came to her mind. When she was a little girl, her *fater* had taken her to the Susquehanna River in March to see the ice go out. It had been an amazing experience to watch the great, white, bluish-tinted pieces of ice jostle one another to make their way down the river. The sense of power and wonder at this beautiful phenomenon of nature somehow involved a release like the one she found in Ransom's arms.

"I think that you are right," she said finally. "But it is a scary experience."

"Tell me about it," he said ruefully.

She watched his eyes search the kitchen and asked what he was looking for. "Well—I haven't had breakfast yet, to tell you the truth, and I wondered if I might buy a blueberry pie from you. I'm in the mood for pie." They both laughed softly at this, and she shook her head at him.

"Please sit down and I'll get it for you."

"I'm going to take you up on that, little hare."

Beth watched him *geh* and sit at the table and went to gladly cut a piece of blueberry pie. He took a taste and smiled broadly. "Excellent pie, Miss Mast! You seem to have many hidden abilities, including your kissing, I might add."

She blushed and he laughed. She realized that this quiet time in the morning together was a gift,

and she wondered if this was what it was like to love
someone—just to sit in their company and feel peace
and happiness.

"Ach." Ransom grinned. "I can see those feminine
wheels turning in your pretty head. What are you
thinking about?"

"Nothing that bears repeating," she said airily, proud
of herself for being able to talk to him with ease. "I
made some things for the *dollhaus* last *nacht*," she said,
and Ransom nodded with interest.

"It's coming along well and should be finished by
the time we have the work frolic at the cabins. Abel
has been tinkering around with some miniature furniture."

"Would you like to see what I've made?" she asked
shyly.

He smiled at her tenderly. "Of course."

"I'll be right back, then."

Ransom waited patiently for Beth and was surprised when there was a soft knock on the back door.
Thinking it might be Abel with some question about
the work, he went quickly to open the door and was
amazed to see Ryan Mason standing there in the half
light. The *Englischer* was staying with Bishop Umble
for a bit while the cabins were finished.

"Yes?" Ransom asked, feeling jealousy rise up in
his throat. *What is this guy doing at Beth's door this early
in the morning?*

"Ransom." Ryan smiled. "May I come in?"

"I suppose." Ransom widened the door reluctantly,
and the other man entered cheerfully.

"I came to check on Beth," Ryan explained. "I heard there was some trouble for her in the cornfield yesterday."

"What?" Ransom was incredulous. *No one knows that happened but Beth and I* . . .

"You'd be surprised how news travels," Ryan said, as if reading Ransom's mind. "So, how is she?"

Ransom glared at the man. "She's fine."

"Is she? Because I think she was reliving some part of the day of her father's death."

"What? How do you know—"

"Like I said, news travels. And because we are talking about Beth and that day, I've heard that she didn't speak for a while. It's funny how guilt can silence us on one hand but make us scream inside on the other."

"I don't know what you're talking about," Ransom growled softly.

"I mean, guilt and regret are powerful things, and you do know what I'm talking about, Ransom King. You still have the sonogram, don't you?"

Ransom was speechless. No one but *Gott* knew of the small black-and-white picture he had tucked in the Bible he'd brought back from his *grossdauddi*'s. He hadn't looked at it in years, but it was there, ever present in the back of his mind.

Ryan shrugged at his continued silence. "See, you can't speak. You worry what people will think of you, that no one would care for you if they knew, right?"

"Get out." Ransom stepped closer to the other man and longed to beat him with his fists. He had no idea why this anger should be churning so intensely inside him, but he didn't want this odd man near Beth.

"It's okay, Ransom," Ryan said softly. "I won't hurt her and I'll go. I see I've pressed too hard this morning."

Ryan slipped out the door and Ransom stood with his head bowed in the kitchen, frozen by Mason's words and insight. The *Englischer* had turned over rocks in the water of Ransom's mind and the experience was painful. "*Nee*," Ransom said out loud. "I don't want you near Beth."

Beth came back to the kitchen carrying her sewing box. "Ach, I thought I heard you talking with someone."

Ransom crossed the kitchen in two long strides. He stood in front of her and lifted his hands to frame her surprised face. Without preamble, and with the pressing need to somehow keep her safe, he bent his head and kissed her hard. Then, because her lips were so sweet, he softened the kiss and moved to press his forehead against hers. "Ach, Beth," he whispered. "Sweet, sweet little hare." He kissed her again, with deepening passion.

"What is going on here!"

The screech made Ransom's head ring, but he automatically pressed his arms around Beth, feeling her shiver with sudden fear.

He looked over Beth's head and met Rose's furious gaze. He was wondering vaguely how he might explain the situation to shield Beth when Viola joined the fray, looking disheveled in a surprisingly hued purple dressing gown.

"Mother! He—She was kissing him!" Rose screamed the words like a petulant child, clearly hoping to put Beth in the wrong.

Ransom felt Beth move in his arms and he glanced down, seeing her pale face and knowing instinctively that she was about to assume the blame. He pulled her closer.

"Frau Mast, Rose." He kept his words measured. "You've discovered our secret. Beth and I are courting."

Chapter Twenty-Six

Beth had to skip to keep up with his long strides as he threaded his way through mountain laurel and sumac, obviously headed for the creek.

"Why did you say that?" she demanded for the fifth time, but he didn't seem to hear her. Instead, he kept walking fast until the dim roar of the rushing creek became a background noise. Then he turned to her.

"Are you going to answer me?" she asked, slightly breathless.

He reached out a hand and thumbed a strand of hair away from her face, and she swallowed hard. "Ransom?"

"Don't fret, little hare. I admit I shouldn't have said we were courting without your permission, but we can always break it off."

Beth knew a sudden disappointment and turned from him to walk toward the water. "Of course . . ." She knew her voice sounded thin. "That's what you would want."

She didn't expect to find him so close behind her,

and she squeaked when he laid his big hands on her shoulders. She shivered when he put his mouth close to her ear. "What are you saying, sweetheart? That you'd like to court the likes of me?"

She longed to tell him just how much she'd like to court with him, but she stilled when he nipped gently at her earlobe. Longing swirled through her brain and made her body sing. She leaned against him, feeling the length of his legs tense against the back of her dress. But then, she came back to herself, straightening her spine and turning in his arms.

"Of course I'd like to court with you, Ransom King, and so would half the other single *maedels* of Ice Mountain."

She watched his dark eyes blink; then a wry smile played about his lips. "So is that *jah* or *nee*, Beth?"

She clasped her hands together between his body and hers, directly in front of her belly, and she blurted out what came to mind. "You must know that I'm not *gut* courting material. You can see how plump I am . . ." She let the words tumble out on a sigh. "And there's . . . a lot of things you don't know about me."

"More secrets, sweet Beth?"

"*Jah.*"

He inched impossibly closer and she watched him as he closed his eyes. Long lashes feathered on ruddy cheeks, and then he bent and kissed the tip of her nose. She felt slightly foolish when she blushed, but he smiled as he opened his eyes and drank her in.

"Let me tell you a secret," he said in husky tones. "There are far too many sharp edges in this world, too many places where a man can't find rest . . ." She felt him skim his hands down her shoulders and then her arms. "But you, sweetheart, are so wonderfully soft and gently curved. When I touch you, I feel like I'm coming home."

Her breath caught at his amazing words and she leaned into him and lifted her mouth to his, kissing him with sudden confidence. . . .

"Courting? Exactly how much of Sarah's pain tea have I been having?" Aenti Ruth stamped her cane imperiously from her supine position on the Kings' couch and glared at Ransom with a demanding eye.

He smiled at her and reached out to rub Petunia's left ear. "Feeling left out? You can help Beth with proper advice on courting."

Aenti Ruth sniffed as she rubbed Second John's thin coat. "I might at that. I doubt the child knows what she wants for the future."

Ransom allowed for a rare moment of lassitude, then, as he recalled Beth's bold kissing of the morning. Her small tongue had teased at his lips like a busy hummingbird seeking nectar. And he'd complied only too willingly, eager to participate in the mutual sweetness. "Ach, she knows what she wants . . ." he drawled, feeling heated by the memory.

His *aenti* harrumphed impatiently. "Ransom King, where exactly is your head?"

He laughed and leaned over Petunia to kiss the *auld* woman on the cheek. "Some fancies are best left unspoken."

She swatted him away with a gentle hand. "Well,

I'm sure Viola had a fit. She's never wanted anything much for that child save the best of a load of work."

"Let me handle Viola."

He made to move away when she caught his hand and whispered low. "Beth cannot give her heart to you in truth, Ransom, until she's found the recipe for being true to herself."

Aenti Ruth's words were sobering, and he nodded, thinking hard.

The corn leaves seemed gigantic, so large that she was able to hide under them. Perhaps if she were able to stay here forever, no one would find her. She could become part of the dirt. A crow flew overhead, its tar-black feathers reflecting the harshness of the moon's light. She thought the bird saw her, and she drew further under the leaves. The crow screamed, a guttural, cackling sound, and Beth squeezed both fingers into her ears. She determined that the best, maybe the only *thing she could do, was to be silent. . . .*

Beth awoke to find the lantern burning gently in her room. Her jaw hurt, and her bedclothes were stained with perspiration. She remembered the dream, and she remembered hiding in the cornfield the day her *fater* died.

She climbed down the ladder to get a cool drink. She'd somehow managed to slip up to bed without a direct confrontation with Viola or Rose about Ransom's claim that she and he were courting. She made her way quietly, her hands still shaking from the dream, and went to the icebox. Her hand hovered between the lemonade and the jar of apple butter, and she thought of the good, fresh bread tucked neatly into the cupboard. But for the first time, she considered what comfort the apple butter would truly bring. She decided to get a glass of water instead and went back to her room.

In bed, Beth sipped at the water. She thought about Derr Herr being the Living Water that was meant to fill her spirit. She knew, though, that since her *fater*'s death, she had remained disconnected from all the comfort *Gott* was able to bring. But then weariness overtook her. She put the glass on the bedside table, lay down, and slipped into a dreamless sleep.

Ransom couldn't sleep. Ryan Mason's words burned in his brain. What was it about Ice Mountain that gave certain people the ability to look into the past? Ransom understood that the bishop had this gift, but who was Ryan Mason to tell him such things? He threw back the light quilt and got out of bed. The moonlight poured through his bedroom window as he reached for the Bible he'd brought home from his *grossdauddi*'s. He flipped it open slowly, and the small black-and-white paper fell into his hand. He closed his eyes hard, wishing he didn't understand the shadowy life of what might have been that was portrayed in what he held. He opened his eyes and turned the picture over in his fingers. Even in the moonlight, he didn't have to strain to make out the contrast between black and gray. . . .

Eerie voices filtered through his consciousness— the technician's cheerful explanations; Barbara's exultant laughter; his own voice—unsteady maybe, but determined . . . then the screams from the *nacht* in the car . . . as if he could hear both of them crying out. . . . His fingers closed gently on the picture, and he knew for certainty what he had to do. . . .

The morning dawned bright and clear. Beth got up early and went out to the kitchen garden to cut some fresh rhubarb for a deep-dish strawberry rhubarb pie to take to the worksite. She felt as if she was moving in a daze when she thought back to her boldness in kissing Ransom the day before. Of course, all of the nonsense about courting would surely fade, but it felt good to imagine it might happen.

She took the small knife from the garden shelf and went to the rhubarb with its pink-throated leaves and started to cut at the base of a thick stalk. She felt the knife slip in the morning dew and quickly drew her hand back. But it was too late, and red blood spilled down against the pink and green of the vegetable. She sighed to herself, then ran over to the spigot and started rinsing off her fingers. The cut was minor, but the blood running down her hand suddenly made her heart pound. She heard again the horse's scream and remembered the powerful jolt. There was blood, but it wasn't hers, and then she was free again, running, running, running through the cornfields.

"Beth, what are you doing standing there?" It was Viola's voice. Beth snapped back to the present and hastily put her hand behind her back.

"Just getting rhubarb for a pie, Viola."

"For Ransom King?"

"*Nee,*" Beth stuttered, unprepared for Viola's tight voice this early in the morning.

"You may as well be making it for him—now that you're courting, of course."

Beth tried to grasp what she'd thought of the previous *nacht*—that she had *Gott* to help her in times of trouble. But it was hard, and she found herself on shaky spiritual ground as she faced her *stepmamm*.

"I—we . . ." She faltered, and Viola's face took on a distinct look of distaste.

"*Jah* . . . I can only image what 'we' was involved in catching a man such as Ransom. I warned you that you must curb your appetites."

Beth felt the older woman's eyes rake her figure, and then she thought about what Ransom had said about her curves. She straightened her shoulders a bit, and Viola openly frowned at the movement. Her *stepmamm* was poised to berate her further when a man's cheerful voice broke into the momentary silence.

"Frau Mast—Beth, I hope you don't mind me stopping by so early."

Beth turned to see Ryan Mason walking through the wet grass. He had a smile on his face and she couldn't resist smiling in return. The *Englischer*'s presence surely meant that Viola would not speak harshly to her any more at the moment.

"Frau Mast, you have a lovely daughter," he said.

"I do indeed," said Viola, seeming mollified. "But how do you know Rose? Or . . . ach, you mean Beth, of course."

Beth said nothing.

"Ah, yes," Ryan said. "Beth is your stepdaughter. What was your first husband like?"

Beth stared at him, appalled, while Viola stuttered. "My first husband . . . ?"

"Yes, your daughter Rose's father."

"Why—he was fine. Just fine."

Beth realized she had never asked Viola, or Rose, about their life before they came to the Mast house, and here was an *Englischer* boldly putting the question to her *stepmamm*.

"Fine is good." Ryan nodded. "Sometimes. But then, we all say 'fine,' don't we? Like 'How are you?' 'Fine'—or 'How are you feeling?' 'Fine.' But the truth is, many of us are not fine. We're really hurt on the inside somewhere. . . ."

His soft words hung in the air, and Beth stared at Viola, amazed to see the older woman's eyes look as if they sparkled with tears.

"You—you must excuse me, young man. Something seems to have gotten in my eye. And . . ." She turned to *geh*, then stopped. "Ach, and, Beth—hurry on with that pie."

She walked back into the cabin.

Beth stared at Ryan in confusion. "How did you . . . I mean . . . I never thought to ask her . . ."

Ryan smiled. "Don't worry, Beth. It's . . . fine. But I was thinking that we might have a good, old-fashioned pie bake-off to put a bit of money in Olivia Lott's pocket. And because you seem to bake more pies than anyone I've ever known, I'd like to know what you think of the idea?"

She hesitated, and his smile grew. "I've already

cleared the plan with Bishop Umble at breakfast this morning."

"Well, that's all right, then! I think it's a *wunderbaar* idea! We could do it the day of the finishing frolic at the cabins."

"Great plan! I'll just—"

"Mason, what are you doing here?"

Beth looked up to see Ransom rounding the kitchen garden's edge and was surprised by the anger in his voice.

Chapter Twenty-Seven

Ransom was furious, though he also knew he was overreacting. *What harm is there in the* Englischer *talking with Beth in the dew of the morning, when she looks as beautifully flushed as a new rose and . . .*

"Ransom? I was discussing with Beth the plan for a pie bake-off."

Ransom frowned, then saw Beth's confused expression. She came forward and put a hand on his arm. "Is everything all right?"

"You're bleeding!" He caught her small hand in his own, knowing his words had come out more harshly than he'd meant.

"It's nothing," she said. "Do you not like the idea of a pie bake-off? It's to raise money for Olivia Lott and the *kinner*. We—"

"Fine, fine . . ." he muttered, intent on her wound. "Excuse us, Mason. I've got to take care of her hand."

"Surely." The *Englischer* nodded and walked away while Ransom urged Beth up the steps of the porch and into the cabin.

"Ransom . . . it's all right. I'm okay."

But he pulled her inexorably to the kitchen pump and got the water going. "Just hold on a minute,

Beth. Where's your first aid kit? Do you have any bandages?" His heart had started to work harder the second he'd seen the blood, but now he was beginning to feel frantic. He needed to do something— anything—to help her. *To help her* . . .

His feelings must have communicated themselves to her in some way, because she suddenly lifted wet hands to touch his cheeks. "Ransom," she whispered softly. "*Kumme* back. I'm all right. See? It's stopped bleeding already."

He wanted to cry; trapped between the past and the present, he stopped short and turned his head to press his lips against her damp hand. He closed his eyes while he tried to regulate his breathing.

"How do you know, little hare?" he choked out finally. "How do you know what I'm thinking and feeling?"

He opened his eyes and looked down at her, watching her wet her pink lips.

"Ach, Ransom . . . I just do. I–I love you."

He bent to kiss her, wanting to tell her that he felt the same, when a loud screech rudely interrupted them. Rose stamped a rather long, bare foot on the kitchen floor and glared at her stepsister.

"You make me sick, Beth Mast! You love him? Is that what you've been saying to try to catch him? Mamm!"

Ransom blew out a breath of exasperation and would have defended Beth's honor on the spot, but she laid a pleading hand against his shirtfront and shook her head. "*Sei se gut*, Ransom, let's *geh* to the worksite."

"Mamm! She's running away and trying to get Ransom to *geh* with her!"

"Rose! What *en der weldt* are you yelling about?" Viola's voice echoed above the fray. "Honestly, you sound like a *boppli*!"

Ransom was still ready to silence Rose, but he noticed the strange expression on Beth's face as she listened to Viola put her *dochder* in her place for once. Beth looked surprised and confused, and he bent to kiss her tenderly, careless of the other women in the room. . . .

I love you . . . I love you. . . . How could I have said that to him? Beth tried to concentrate on slicing the honey ham in front of her into thin pieces as she worked on assembling sandwiches at the cabin site with Mary Lyons and Lucy.

Her best friend nudged her when she started to slow down production. "Beth." Lucy giggled. "You just put that slice of ham in the horseradish mustard jar."

Beth felt herself flush. "I'm sorry." She glanced past Lucy to find Mary's eyes full of warmth and kindness.

"I remember when I first began to think of Jude . . . well, I still think of him, and it distracts me."

Beth felt the other women laugh with her and risked taking a glance at the spot where Ransom was poised on the side of one of the roofs, a hammer in his hand and a nail in his firm mouth. *Everything about him seems tantalizing.* Even in a simple white shirt and dark pants, he caused her heart to beat faster and whatever was before her eyes to melt away in pleasant reflection . . . especially when she was thinking about his kisses.

"Word's gotten around, Beth," Lucy said happily.

"About you and Ransom courting. *Kumme* this fall, I expect we'll be sisters in truth as well as heart."

"Ach, I . . ." Beth knew that courting, normally done in secret, would usually result in marriage for a couple. But she wasn't even sure if she and Ransom were truly courting. It was all very confusing. . . . She was saved from having to make a proper reply when Bishop Umble stopped by with his cheerful blue eyes snapping.

"Ladies, have you heard about the pie bake-off during the finishing frolic? Coming up fast, I think. The cabins are nearly done, and I think we're set to have the frolic next Thursday. Hope to see you all here! Ach, and Beth, Ransom tells me that you are the finest baker of pies he knows!"

"*Danki*," Beth murmured, feeling distinctly uncomfortable with the focus of the bishop's conversation being on her and her baking.

But everyone laughed good-naturedly, and Beth swallowed, then relaxed. She wasn't used to praise, yet she knew it was all right to drink in a compliment now and then.

She realized that Bishop Umble was still speaking and she dragged her attention back from her inner thoughts.

"Well, that's a fine thing, Beth! Just what a man needs. I'll leave you to it!"

"What? I—" But the genial spiritual leader had moved on, leaving Beth with no idea what she'd gotten herself in to. . . .

"You're going to fall through that roof, little *bruder*, if you don't keep your mind on your work!"

Jeb's teasing voice drifted up to Ransom, and he looked down between the cabin's beams to smile at his older *bruder*. He took the nail out of his mouth.

"And just where do you think my mind is, Jeb?"

Jeb looked away, then grinned back up at him. "Here's someone who might be able to answer that question."

Ransom watched his *bruder* sweep off his hat, then hurry away as Beth's charming figure came into view. "Hello, sweetheart," he called down.

She peered up at him, her blue eyes wide. "Shhh . . . you don't have to say that, Ransom."

He slipped his hammer into his tool belt. "Say what, Beth Mast?"

She looked at him as she probably would a naughty child, and something impish and fun, long subdued, took hold of him. He crawled backward down the slope of the roof, then shimmied down the wide logs to swing himself to the ground.

She frowned up at him. "You don't need to call me sweetheart."

"I think I should call my courting *maedel* anything beautiful that I like, and 'sweetheart' fits you perfectly."

He watched her exhale and he caught her close. "Ransom," she squeaked. "Everyone will see and besides . . . Bishop Umble said I should give you this."

"A *buss*, sweet Beth?"

"*Nee.*" She swung a small jug from behind her back.

"Moonshine?" he queried with a laugh.

"*Nee.* Here. Take it, if you please."

"Surely." He accepted the jug and uncorked the lid with curiosity. Then he lifted the crockery and drank deeply.

He drank for several seconds, then swung down the jug and grinned. He pulled her close once more as he lowered his cream-covered lips to capture her mouth.

Beth tasted the creamy eggnog and cinnamon and nutmeg from his mouth as he kissed her without reservation. All thought of anyone watching slipped from her mind as she reached to twine her arms about his neck.

"Is it Christmas *kumme* early, then, sweet Beth?" Ransom asked when he stopped to take a breath.

"You know all the women on Ice Mountain give their men—uh—I mean—" She stumbled over her words and felt herself blush when the dimple appeared beside his firm mouth.

"You mean I'm your man?"

Now what have I gotten myself in to? But jah, *oh* jah, *you are, you are. . . .* "I wasn't thinking," she finally said a bit primly.

He laughed, but then his dark eyes suddenly grew serious, and she worried she had overstepped some boundary with him.

"*Kumme,* sweetheart, I've got to make sure of the count of two-by-fours that are stored in a barn I believe you know well."

"Ransom—I can't," she whispered.

"*Danki,* sweetheart! And we can finish off the eggnog there too." He caught her hand, and she would have resisted, but others around them laughed gently in accord with Ransom.

They passed Olivia Lott and she smiled at them.

Beth noticed that some of the sadness had lifted from her eyes and face.

"Going to have lunch?" The *Englischwoman* asked.

Beth winced when Ransom replied with ease, "Something like that!"

They entered the green woods and soon reached the supply barn. Ransom slid the door open, and Beth saw him give a quick look about before he pulled her inside and slid the door closed.

Beth noticed immediately that there was an intimacy about the silence of the place. Dust motes played in long sunbeams and cobwebs glistened in far corners. She looked up at him, ready to scold him for his boldness in bringing her to the barn, but she couldn't find the heart to do it. If truth be told, she wanted to be with him—anywhere he was. Then she watched Ransom put down the eggnog jug on a bale of hay, and he turned to look at her with a gravity that belied any previous playacting.

"Beth, there's something I need to show you. I've been waiting for the right time, and just now, when I thought you were calling me your man—you have to know before you start thinking like that."

"I'm sorry for what I said, Ransom. You don't need to show me anything. I understand."

But he merely shook his head and pulled a carefully folded piece of white paper from his pocket, then held it out to her.

Beth reached hesitant fingers to his own and accepted the paper but didn't look at it as Ransom began to speak. "Beth, I told you a little about Barbara, but not the truth."

He looked away, and she watched him visibly

struggle with what he seemed to need to say. "Beth—
I . . . *Sei se gut*, look at what you hold."

Beth nodded and slowly began to unfold the
paper. She realized that it was a photo of some sort,
which seemed strange, because their people normally
didn't keep or take photos.

She unfolded it completely, then turned it over
with care. She moved to stand in a sunbeam so she
could see better. The black and gray colors looked
grainy, and the strange circle in the middle was both
alien and familiar to her consciousness.

"What is it?" she whispered.

"A baby—a sonogram picture."

"It–it's Barbara's *boppli*?" She asked the question
even as the answer dawned on her. "Barbara's and . . .
yours?"

Chapter Twenty-Eight

"*Jah*. Our baby."

"You were married?"

He shook his head, realizing that now he had started to tell the truth, he meant to finish. "I wanted her to marry me. I was seventeen and she was twenty. She . . . was . . . happy, I guess, about the pregnancy, because it was a way, she thought, to escape her parents' control of her life, but I don't think she loved the baby . . . not truly. . . ."

"Where is your baby?"

Ransom thought it odd that so simple a question could so easily reduce him to tears. He blinked them back and swallowed hard. "One *nacht* . . . we were in Barbara's car. She was driving, and she was screaming at me about wanting to leave Ohio. She said that if I wouldn't take her, she had an *Englischer* who would. She lost control of the car . . . we hit a tree. The engine exploded into flames. I got out and ran around to her side of the car. It . . . she was screaming. There was a lot of blood and the car seemed . . . mangled around her. I tried to open the door . . . By then someone else had stopped, and then the police and rescue people, but it was too late. Barbara died . . . the baby died . . . and I think that part of me died too."

Beth carefully held the sonogram in her hand; it was as though the picture cried out to her. So much promise, so much of what might have been . . . and then to lose your beloved in such a way. . . . She shuddered, and Ransom must have seen her and misunderstood.

"I don't blame you for how you must feel about me, Beth. I might have reasoned with her—taken the wheel—something, but I failed. I failed them both, and I don't want to fail someone like that again."

"You mean me?" Beth asked quietly.

"*Jah.*"

He sounded miserable and she longed to comfort him, but she knew she couldn't ever take the place of the ghosts of his past. She handed him the sonogram and spoke softly. "I understand." Then she whirled and ran to the barn door, sliding it open in a haze of tears. She wanted to be alone.

Ransom wanted to follow her, but he'd seen the stricken expression on her beautiful face. He folded the sonogram and eased it back into his front pocket; then he too prepared to leave the barn.

He'd almost reached the open door when a flurry of apron, *kapp* strings, and dark blond hair flew in through the door frame like a bird from a storm. Beth looked up at him, a bit wild-eyed. "I have a secret too, Ransom. One that I've never told anyone—one that only *Gott* knows."

"Shhh." He tried to soothe her. "It's all right, little hare. You share so much with me every day—you needn't share your secret unless you truly want to."

"I do, ach, I do, Ransom. I nearly told you that day in the cornfield, but I ran out of courage."

She hiccupped on a sob and he gathered her close, longing to assuage her grief. "Then share my courage, sweetheart, such as it is. . . ."

He bent and kissed her and she returned his kisses eagerly. He reached to ease the door shut behind her and found it stuck for some reason. He glanced up to see Ryan Mason holding the door open with a firm hand.

"Ransom, Beth. Sorry to interrupt."

"It seems you've got quite a knack for interrupting lately," Ransom said with a frown as he pulled a disheveled Beth behind him to hide her from Mason's keen eyes.

"It's all right, Ransom." Beth sniffed. "I'll speak with you another time."

Ryan Mason smiled. "Now, that will solve my problem perfectly."

"What do you mean?" Ransom asked with impatience.

"Olivia Lott mentioned how much she and her children love to read, so the bishop and I thought that some built-in bookcases might be a nice touch in the largest cabin. I wondered if you might do some measuring and consult about the design."

Ransom sighed to himself. He had no desire to leave Beth shaken and alone and was about to tell Mason so when Beth spoke up clearly. "Ransom, it's all right. Truth be told, I was going to head home early today. It's Viola's birthday and I've got a lot to prepare for her supper." She stepped out from behind him, and he saw that she'd tidied her hair and had her *kapp* in proper order. Only her cheeks looked tearstained, but she visibly straightened her spine and made to *geh* when Ryan Mason offered his arm to her.

"Beth, I'd be honored to walk you back."

Ransom glared at the other man as Beth put her small hand on Mason's arm. "I can walk her back myself."

But Beth shook her head. "*Nee*, Ransom, *sei se gut*, *geh* and help the bishop. I'll be fine."

Mason flashed him a smile and turned to go with Beth, leaving Ransom to stare after them, worried for her. . . .

Beth concentrated on beating the mayonnaise cake icing, stirring until her arm hurt and the sugar dissolved. She set the blue mixing bowl aside with a sigh, then checked on the rich chocolate cake, which still had to cool a bit before she could ice it. She was making one of Viola's favorite meals—pork chops with stuffing, sugared carrots, and mashed potatoes with brown onion gravy.

She checked on the pork chops, then went to set the table. She used the simple pale blue plates and the cloth napkins, which she'd embroidered herself for Viola's last birthday, then added the silverware—worn to almost delicate thinness after having been in Viola's family for years. Beth poured ice water into glasses from a metal pitcher, then went out to the side of the porch to pick some trailing pink roses to add to the birthday table. She reentered the kitchen through the screen door and thought of Ransom. *His secret* . . . She felt tears well up in the corners of her eyes and hastily brushed them aside with the hem of her apron.

She had wanted to tell him her own secrets, but Ryan had interrupted . . . Ryan Mason made her feel both safe and unsure at the same time. The simple youth minister seemed to have Bishop Umble's gift for seeing beyond what the normal eye could take in. He'd talked with her casually as they'd walked back from the cabin construction site; then he'd mentioned the conversation he'd had with Viola about her first husband. His words caused Beth to see her *stepmamm* in a different light, one that illuminated what the past might have been like during her first marriage.

Beth was wiping at the kitchen counter when Rose came in without returning her greeting. Her stepsister sat down at the pretty table with her back to Beth, and Beth tried to ignore the obvious insult.

Beth turned and thoughtfully rubbed the dishcloth in circles against the wood of the counter, then drew a deep breath. "Rose? Do you remember what your *fater* was like?" Beth didn't turn, didn't want to face the rejection Rose would probably express. But to Beth's surprise, silence reigned in the kitchen for a few moments; then Rose's voice came, hesitant and childlike.

"He was mean."

Beth turned slowly and slipped into a seat at the table across from Rose. "He was—mean?"

Rose nodded, reaching to fiddle with the petals of the rose nearest her. "My first memory is of him screaming. Always screaming." She crushed the petal between her fingers. "He was mean to Mamm too, but we've never talked about it. Why do you want to know?"

Beth thought of Ryan Mason and the way he had asked Viola the same question in the very same place. *What is it about speaking the truth? Asking for truth that reveals so much in our lives?* Beth reached across the table and patted Rose's arm. "I wanted to know because I realize I never thought about what your life was like with your other *fater* and . . ." She didn't know how to go on. "Do you want to *geh* for a walk after supper? We could—talk."

Rose frowned. "*Nee* . . . I don't want to talk to you, and besides, you'll have to attend to the cleaning up." She flounced from the table, leaving Beth to thoughtfully gather the strewn rose petals.

Ransom had the odd sensation that a great weight had been lifted from his back, and a cascade of memories assailed his senses. He remembered things that gave him pleasure, things long forgotten, from before the accident that had so defined him. Holding a lathe for the first time, the sheen of a rainbow trout, summer meadows and cutting trees, the clean scent of pine and the roll of thunder over the mountain. . . . All of this and more rushed at him, and he knew it was because he'd shared the truth with Beth. He'd risked exposing the worst about himself and had found liberation in the process. Truth. For so long, he had made it a relative thing, unwilling to face its power and preferring to be a slave to the lies he felt he had to keep telling.

And then he remembered what the Bible said: "The truth shall set you free."

Beth bowed her head for silent grace as she prepared to eat the birthday supper with Viola and Rose. She tried to focus her thoughts on blessings for Viola, but then breathed prayers for Ransom and his past as well. She knew that he had entrusted her with the truth, and the courage and humility that took humbled her.

"Beth, for the third time, pass the carrots." Rose's petulant voice cut through her thoughts, and she looked up, realizing that both Viola and her stepsister were regarding her with less than kindly eyes.

"Ach, sorry. I was thinking—" She reached for the carrot dish and almost dropped it before she consciously steadied her hand.

"Thinking about Ransom, no doubt." Viola's voice was dry.

Something made Beth lift her chin at her *stepmamm*'s confrontational tone. "*Jah*, I was. Do you like the pork chops, Viola? I think they're especially tender." Beth's heart beat fast; she couldn't believe she'd spoken so firmly.

Indeed, Viola raised a gray eyebrow, as if she couldn't believe it either. "Perhaps so much time at the worksite has made you forget your manners, Beth?"

Again, a surge of something daring made Beth respond with unusual clearness. "*Nee*, I've only learned *gut* things about folks there, Viola. It has blessed me in many ways."

"Mamm, can you listen to me instead of Beth?"

Rose broke into the conversation. "I really need a new dress for the work frolic and pie bake-off."

Beth watched Viola's eyes shift in her *dochder*'s direction. "Why, of course, Rose. We will *geh* to Ben Kauffman's tomorrow for the fabric. Beth, you will stay home from the cabin site tomorrow so you can sew Rose's dress. And Rose, you must, of course, make a pie for the contest. There's a donation fee for entering. Beth, I don't think you'll have time to bake because you'll be making Rose's dress."

Beth swallowed in disappointment and didn't feel so bold anymore. She took a small bite of carrots and nodded. "*Jah*, Viola. I will do as you say."

Chapter Twenty-Nine

Ransom rose early and washed at the bowl and pitcher on his dresser before pulling on a light green shirt and raising his suspenders. He'd had a great *nacht*'s sleep and felt cheerful as he entered the kitchen to the delightful smell of bacon frying and the sight of blueberry pancakes rising on the griddle. He bent and *bussed* his *mamm* on the cheek, then snatched a piece of bacon and turned away. Esther was setting the table and he caught her around the waist for a quick hug.

"What *en der weldt* is wrong with your head, Ransom King?" she snapped at him, squeaking when he twirled her about.

"Nothing is wrong. I just think it's a *gut* day, that's all!"

He left his sister to bend and pet Petunia, who was nosing about the kitchen.

"Huh!" Aenti Ruth snorted from the couch. "The *buwe*'s in love, that's what!"

Ransom laughed. "Your ankle must be feeling better and I'm glad for that!"

Second John briefly howled in agreement as

Ransom went to the couch to see his *aenti*. He bent and gave her wrinkled cheek a quick kiss and she swatted him away, though he could tell she was touched. "Stop your foolishness, Ransom. It's wasted on an *auld* woman. Save your kisses for sweet Beth."

"Liiike her," Jack squawked.

"Perhaps, little bird," he agreed with *gut* humor.

"I want some licorice," Aenti Ruth said. "Do you have the time to stop off at Kauffman's?"

"I'll do it right after breakfast."

"*Gut.* Make sure it's black. I don't go for that red stuff."

"Black licorice it is, Aenti Ruth."

He ate quickly, then left the *haus*, waved at his *daed* in the workshop, and set off for the general store.

He climbed the white steps of Kauffman's, welcoming the barrage of scents that hit him when he entered the store. The smells of freshly ground coffee, old wood floors, newly baked bread, tanned leather, and a hundred other scents played like musical notes in the tasty air.

Ransom threaded his way through friends who were shopping and made it to the counter of large glass jars filled with the bright colors of various candies—peppermint and wintergreen, lollipops and wafer spaceships. It all looked *gut.*

"What'll you have, Herr King?" One of Ben's sons, Eli, gave him a gap-toothed smile from behind the counter.

"Ach, five licorice pipes, *sohn.* The black ones." He was watching the child carefully put the candy in a small brown bag when he heard his name called in sugared tones.

"Ransom King, you're up early."

He turned with a faint sigh to face Rose and nodded politely. "*Gut* morning."

She caught his arm and stepped intimately close to him. He longed to shake her off like a bug, but he reminded himself that she was part of Beth's family; instead, he followed her obediently to the fabric counter.

He caught the eye of Clara, Ben Kauffman's elderly sister, as she stood with shears poised over an array of different colored material. The older woman gave him a sour smile, then rolled her eyes in Rose's direction, but the girl was impervious. She held Ransom's arm closer to the side of her breast and wriggled in obvious excitement.

"I'm having a new dress made for the frolic and pie bake-off, Ransom, and I can't decide what color. What do you think?"

I think Beth is probably making your dress. . . . He moved away from Rose a bit and stifled his negative thoughts. "The dark green is *gut*," he said finally, trying to be objective.

"Ach, Ransom, *jah*, the forest green will *geh* so well with my red hair! You understand women, don't you?"

Ransom clutched the bag of licorice pipes in a death grip as Clara put her shears to good work, cutting the yardage. "*Danki*, Rose." He moved to extract himself from her grip, but she practically pinned his back to the shelf of homemade jams. Clara looked up once with a dour expression, and Ransom longed for the moment to be over.

"I must tell you a secret," Rose whispered, then stood on tiptoe to cup her hand about his ear. "My pie will be blueberry with a lattice top and a heart right in the center . . . just in case you might forget."

"Okay."

Ransom wondered briefly how Rose had discovered that Bishop Umble had asked him to be one of the three judges at the pie bake-off. But he dismissed the thought when Rose began to flutter about him excitedly, like some gaudy butterfly. *Ach, how much I prefer Beth's quiet and peaceful nature. . . . A girl like Rose makes my head hurt.* He eased away from her and nodded to Clara before making a hasty exit through the front door. Once outside, he drew in a refreshing breath of summer air and wondered how Beth could put up with such a sister.

Beth gently unwrapped the brown paper from the forest green fabric that Rose had brought home earlier that morning.

"Ransom picked it out for me," Rose cooed as she ate a fresh blueberry muffin. "He has such *gut* taste. I tell you, Beth, I think your whole courting scheme is just a cover for Ransom to be able to see me more often."

Beth stared at her stepsister, feeling as though her head was spinning. *What if Rose's chatter is true?* But then she straightened her back as she remembered the look on Ransom's face when he told her of the baby and Barbara.

"Think what you like, Rose," she said coolly, looking back down at the material in front of her.

Rose flicked at Beth's *kapp* string as she passed by.

"I will think what I like, stepsister, and you be sure that my dress is finished in time for the frolic."

Beth pressed her lips together hard and was thankful to *Gott* that she managed to hold her tongue and keep her temper, though hot words boiled in the back of her mind. She regained her composure and opened her sewing basket. She knew how to make dresses for Rose; she'd done it far too many times in the past.

She cut the pattern carefully, then looked up as she heard Viola's voice raised in the living room. Her *stepmamm* was scolding Thumbelina, and Beth felt a surge of anger as she abandoned her sewing.

"Is Thumbelina doing something to bother you, Viola?"

"Naturally," Viola replied. "That cat is nothing but a nuisance."

"That cat is my friend," Beth said with sudden asperity.

Thumbelina ran toward Beth as if he knew she was defending him. Beth caught up the old cat in her arms and rubbed her cheek against his fur.

Viola looked as surprised as Beth felt in her contradiction of her *stepmamm*, but Beth would not have Thumbelina treated poorly.

"Perhaps I should *geh* up to my room for a bit with him, Viola."

"And leave Rose's dress? I don't think so." She pursed her lips. "I'll not trouble with the cat any further."

For Beth, it was a small victory, but one she had to confess to *Gott* as she went back to her sewing. She had *nee* desire to be sly but, ach, she was so happy that Thumbelina would not be troubled any further that morning.

Ransom paused in his hammering to listen to Bishop Umble as the *auld* leader paused by the nearly finished bookshelves in the main cabin.

"Nice work here, Ransom."

"*Danki*, Bishop."

"I heard through the Amish grapevine that Beth is not to join us today."

"I figured as much. She's probably at the cabin sewing a dress for Rose to wear to the frolic."

"Hmmm . . . Well, Olivia Lott wanted to see her. Perhaps you might take Olivia to the Mast cabin later this afternoon?"

With Viola and Rose there? "With Viola and Rose there?" He said the unspoken words aloud and had the grace to look abashed when Bishop Umble raised a gray eyebrow.

"*Jah.*" The *auld* leader stroked his beard. "Perhaps it might be helpful for all involved."

Ransom wanted to turn away from the knowing blue eyes, but instead, he nodded. "All right. *Jah,* I'll take her."

"*Gut* man. Lucy will watch the *kinner* here. I'll tell Olivia."

"*Gut.*" *Just* gut . . . *great. Now I have to show the* Englischwoman *just how screwed up an Amish household can be. . . .*

Beth reached a hand behind her head to ease the ache in her neck that came from bending over sewing so long. She had basted all the seams and knew it was ready for Rose to be fitted properly, but she hadn't been troubled by her stepsister for a few hours and had to admit that the neck strain was worth the afternoon of peace.

She sighed and rose to get a glass of water when she heard horse hooves on the dirt road outside. Her heart started beating fast when she saw Ransom's handsome profile, and she regretted the perspiration stains she knew marked the underarms of her dress. But her self-consciousness was quickly dismissed in her pleasure at the chance to see him. She hurried to the front door of the cabin and pushed to open the screen. Thumbelina wound himself around her legs and Beth smiled at the sight of Ransom helping Olivia Lott down from the wagon seat.

"Beth, do we have visitors?"

Beth's heart sank at the sound of Viola's voice behind her. "*Jah.*"

"Well, don't just stand there, girl. . . . Allow me to greet them while you clean up your sewing."

Beth bent and scooped up Thumbelina, then brushed past Viola to return to the half-made dress. She put Thumbelina down gently and began to carefully fold the fabric that was spread out on the table.

"Hello, Frau Mast, this is Olivia Lott. She wonders if she might speak to Beth . . . and I'd like to see her for a moment or two myself."

"Beth has been sewing for her stepsister. She must do it, dear child, because she knows how delicate Rose can be. . . ."

Beth felt her face suffuse with color as she heard Viola speak the lie so sweetly.

"I see." Ransom's tone was hollow, and Beth wanted to hug him for so obviously doubting Viola.

"But do *kumme* in," Viola went on. "I'll fetch Rose."

Beth didn't look up when Viola walked past her, nor did she move when she sensed that Ransom had *kumme* to stand close to her.

"Leave this sewing, sweet Beth." He gently took the green material from her hands.

"You chose a perfect color," she whispered back, raising her eyes to meet his.

A smile tugged at the corners of his mouth. "I did, didn't I?"

She had to smile in return and forgot about Olivia, Violet, and Rose as he bent to kiss her once. She felt dazed for a moment and was full of bliss, even when Viola and Rose came back to the kitchen.

"If you'll forgive me, Frau Mast—Rose." Ransom cleared his throat. "Olivia and I are to share a picnic lunch with Beth down by the creek. Martha Umble sent the basket along, and the bishop said you would surely understand, given the pleasant friendship Beth and Olivia have formed."

Beth didn't look to see the expression on Viola's face, but she knew *her stepmamm* could hardly be happy. But in this, she seemed to be mistaken, as Viola spoke with an understanding nod. "Why, *jah*, of course. I would never stand in the way of the bishop's plans, but dear Mrs. Lott, please allow me to sit with you a moment and offer my condolences on the loss of your husband. I too lost my husband in a terrible accident, and I feel, as widows, that we might share in the comfort of surviving."

Beth drew a sharp breath. Against her will, words filled her mind. *It was my* fater, *not only your husband.*

And I survived. I survived too . . . Why? Why? The thoughts were too much for her on top of the already tense situation, and Beth mumbled a hasty apology, then ran blindly out the screened door. . . .

Ransom was torn between leaving Olivia with the two obviously scheming women and going after Beth. But then Olivia gave him a brisk wink and a slight nod of her head. Clearly, the *Englischwoman* felt she could hold her own, so he turned and walked out the door.

A slight movement near the door of the barn caught his eye and he followed quickly. It was warm inside the sheep barn, and it took a few moments for him to locate Beth until he heard some muffled sobbing from behind a mound of fresh hay.

He rounded the hay and saw that she'd thrown herself down like a hurt child and was weeping into the crook of her arm. He sank down beside her, waiting until she'd cried herself quiet before gently leaning over her and stroking her back.

"Little hare, will you tell me what troubles you so? Viola mentioned your *fater*'s death and then you ran. . . ."

She nodded, then rolled to her back to stare up at him with brimming blue eyes. "*Jah*," she whispered. "My *fater* died and I didn't."

Ransom wiped at the tracks of her tears with the back of his hand. "Is that your secret, sweet Beth? That you feel guilty for being the one who walked away? Because you know I understand."

She shook her head, squeezing her eyes tightly

shut. "*Nee*," she choked. "I didn't walk away. I caused the accident. I killed my *fater*. . . ."

Beth opened her eyes, expecting to see condemnation and shock on his face, but instead, his dark gaze held steady and calm.

"You were thirteen," he said softly. "Will you tell me what happened?"

"My *fater* took me on an outing to Coudersport . . ." She swallowed hard, feeling the words burn the back of her throat. "We had a *gut* time, but I–I was hungry on the way back." *I could feel the sun on my face and see the lunch pail, a silver bucket covered by a white napkin, on the floor of the buggy near my* fater*'s feet*. "I was hungry and didn't want to wait to picnic near the Ice Mine. I–I grew impatient with my *fater* and reached . . . reached for the lunch pail myself. The napkin blew off the top and flew by the horse's face." *I followed the dance of the pretty white napkin, linen against pale blue sky—beautiful in unfolded flight*. "But then the horse reared, startled by the napkin. My *fater* lost the reins and the horse came down hard. I–I think it broke its leg, because it screamed. The buggy tipped and I was thrown out into a field. I saw my *daed* tumble from the buggy seat into the horse's slashing hooves. There was blood and . . . and I still held the lunch pail. I ran and ran until I came to a cornfield. I didn't want to be found. My gluttony killed my *fater*. I wanted to die. I think I still want to sometimes. . . . That's why I eat most when I'm alone, I suppose."

She stopped and drew a deep breath. She realized the telling of her secret had purged some of the poison from her mind. She listened to Ransom's breathing—slow and even in the sudden quiet; then she swiped her hand over her face and he kissed her forehead gently. "Thank you, little hare. *Danki* for trusting me with your secret. That took courage, sweet Beth. A lot of courage and a lot of love from *Gott*."

She drank in his words like spring water and kissed him gently in return.

Chapter Thirty

For the Amish of Ice Mountain, a work frolic combined the elements of building and fun to benefit the whole community or, in this case, the Lotts and whoever else *Gott* led to rest at Ice Mountain.

Ransom gladly helped Aenti Ruth into the back of the wagon among a clutch of comfortable pillows and elevated her still-sore foot. His *mamm* was there to hold the injured ankle steady while his brother Abel made sure Aenti Ruth's animal family didn't become overly rambunctious.

"Mind that package I gave you, Ransom," Aenti Ruth called over Second John's yips. "It's a gift for your Beth."

My Beth . . . My Beth . . . He tasted the words and found them to be a delight. He thought back to the moments the day before in the barn, when Beth had shared with him the secret that gnawed at her heart. He had wanted to tell her that everything would be all right, but he knew that healing from such a wound would take time.

"Daydreaming, Ransom?" Aenti Ruth's acerbic tone cut into his thoughts, and he turned to smile at the *auld* woman.

"That I am!" It was funny that he had no problem admitting how he felt now. He knew that the process of sharing their secrets with each other had actually brought Beth and him closer together. And he knew that *Gott*'s Hand was on him . . . and on her.

He loosened the brake and had begun to turn the horse when Aenti Ruth cried out sharply, "Ransom! Stop! Second John just took off after a squirrel!"

He muttered to himself as he reset the brake and turned in time to see the dog's hindquarters disappear into the woods. "He'll *kumme* back, I'm sure."

Ransom's mother murmured in agreement, but his *aenti* was having none of it. "I cannot *geh* to the frolic until he's safe and sound." Her aged voice broke for a moment, and Ransom's frustration at the situation eased.

"All right, Aenti Ruth. I'll *geh* and fetch him back. You sit tight with Mamm. Abel, *kumme* sit in the driver's seat." He jumped down from the high wagon seat and headed off into the woods.

"Beth! The hem on this dress is too long. How could you make such a mistake?" Rose's wail echoed throughout the cabin.

Beth turned a placid but tired face to her stepsister and glanced at the offending hem. "The length is fine, Rose. You look quite beautiful."

"*Jah*, you do," Viola said, coming into the bedroom. "And you'd best *geh* and check your pie. It should be nearly done."

Rose gave a huffing response and brushed past Beth to go to the kitchen.

"Really, Beth," Viola said. "You look an absolute

mess. And the kitchen—why there's lard practically rubbed into the counters. You're going to have to stay behind until you finish cleaning up and then walk to the frolic. I really don't know what's *kumme* over you."

"Viola," Beth replied softly, "Rose left the kitchen the way it is while she was baking her pie."

Her *stepmamm* sniffed. "*Gott* calls on us to share one another's burdens, Beth. It doesn't matter who made the mess; you will clean it up."

Beth nodded, but she knew now, with stark clarity, that her *stepmamm* treated her unfairly.

At first, Ransom heard the yipping of Second John nearby and jogged after the little dog, but then the barking faded and he groaned at the thought of the pup making its way down the mountain somewhere. Still, the catch in Aenti Ruth's aged voice echoed in his brain, and he picked up speed while calling for the dog.

Viola and Rose had gone, and Beth breathed a sigh of relief even as she scrubbed the sticky kitchen counters with lemon water. She let her thoughts drift to the day before, when she'd told Ransom her secret. His handling of what had tormented her for so long—with gentle kisses and reassurances—had made her feel cocooned with love. She knew that his response, through Derr Herr, had given her the quiet strength she needed to stand up to Viola about who had actually made the mess in the kitchen.

She finished the pile of dirty dishes, then briefly

went outside to shake out her white apron. She sighed as she reentered the *haus*. Viola and Rose had kept her so busy, she had not had time to bake a pie of her own to enter in the contest. She told herself that it didn't matter and climbed the loft ladder to her cramped room. It was muggy, and she quickly decided she would wear the dress Ransom had liked but Viola had criticized—the blueberry dress, as he had called it.

She lifted it from its neat folds at the bottom of her chest, then turned to her dresser to briefly look in the mirror as she donned a fresh *kapp*. It was then that her eyes happened to catch on the secret drawer hidden within the scrollwork; it was slightly ajar, and she knew with a sudden intuition that its contents were gone. She lifted the lid to be sure and did not see the recipe Aenti Ruth had given her. Immediately, she thought of Rose—childish Rose, who could not bear not knowing all that went on beneath the roof of the cabin. Beth sighed, replaced the wood carefully, then headed down the ladder, prepared to walk to the frolic.

She had just stepped outside onto the front porch when the distinct and terrible smell of skunk permeated her senses. The odor was so strong, she could practically taste it. A moment later, Second John was yelping and whining as he made his way, half-blinded, toward Beth. Obviously, the young dog had run off and tangled with the wrong end of a skunk. Beth pitied him but tried to keep his muddy paws away from the clean blue of her dress. But the dog insisted on jumping up again and again, finally leaving both the smell and a dozen footprints all over her dress and apron.

She gave up the idea of getting to the frolic anytime soon and picked up the suffering dog, heading for the nearest porch beam and collecting a length of clothesline along the way. She tied Second John there, then went down into the root cellar to get as many jars of canned tomatoes as she could carry and came back up into the sunshine to find Second John howling piteously. She set the jars on the porch steps, then went over to the barn to get the large metal tub she used to bathe the sheep. She put the dog in the tub and began to empty the jars of tomatoes and juice, pouring them all over the hapless victim. Second John was surprisingly cooperative, almost as if he sensed she was trying to help. She knelt as she worked the tomatoes into his wiry fur and tried to wash his muzzle without getting tomato juice into his dark eyes.

"Now let this be a lesson to you, friend. Leave the skunks alone." Her tone was light and she started to whistle softly.

"You've got the best attitude of any girl I know."

Beth turned in surprise at Ransom's compliment. She made to get up, then thought better of it as Second John began to squirm. "All right. All right," she soothed, focusing once more on the little dog.

Out of the corner of her eye, though, she didn't miss the fact that Ransom had stripped off his shirt, revealing his tanned, well-defined chest and belly. He put the shirt on the porch chair, then knelt on the other side of the tub, plunging his big hands into the squishy tomatoes. Beth glanced up once to his collarbone, then quickly looked away. Even though she knew she was a sight, she found Ransom's body to be entrancing and she could feel her cheeks warm despite the odd situation.

"It's the same for me, sweet Beth," he said softly, and she met his eyes without thinking.

"Wh–what?"

"Seeing your body—I like to . . . imagine what lies beneath the apron, the dress, the shift. . . ."

Beth felt her mouth form a soft "O" of surprise, but, at the same time, she also knew a flame of response deep in her belly. But she was saved from making any response when Second John suddenly broke free and jumped from the tub to begin to shake as only a wet dog drenched in tomatoes can. . . .

Ransom didn't miss the shy lift, then downward sweep of her honey-colored lashes, even as he pulled her, laughing, to her feet. He forgot about where they were and bent forward to kiss her with slow, sultry sips of her sweet lips. He let his tongue do a wet, languid dance with hers and his hands moved of their own accord to lightly skim her shoulders, then slide to her lower back, pulling her close.

"Ach, Beth . . . I want . . . I mean, I . . ."

"I–I think I want too . . ." Her soft admission set off fireworks behind his eyes, and the summer sun seemed to burn with an intensity beyond hot. *I can't remember feeling like this with Barbara. . . .* The thought both spurred him on and reminded him that he was risking a young girl's purity. . . . *No matter how much she wants . . .*

Ransom came back to his senses in time to hear a wagon making its way down the dirt road near the Mast cabin. He hastily straightened and pulled Beth behind him as Second John began to bark and wriggle in welcome.

"Whoo-ee, big *bruder*!" Abel called from the high seat. "You stink."

"Not a way to approach a lady, Abel," Ransom drawled with good humor. He realized that his *mamm* and Aenti Ruth must have gotten tired of waiting for him to find the dog and had *kumme* searching themselves.

"I'd best *geh* and change," Beth said, easing away from him.

"Don't let that sweet *maedel geh* just yet, Ransom," Aenti Ruth hollered from the back of the wagon. "Not until she's opened the gift I have for her."

Ransom now recalled the brown-paper-wrapped package Abel handed down to him, and he held it out to Beth.

"*Danki.*" Beth smiled, charming despite the splat of tomato juice on her right cheek. "Should I open it?"

Ransom saw Aenti Ruth wave a negligent hand. "You're welcome, child, but open it up inside when you've finished cleaning up. We'll wait here to take you to the frolic, and Ransom can get his shirt back on properly."

Ransom smiled good-naturedly, then walked Beth to the porch and grabbed up his shirt. He couldn't resist studying the movement of her curved hips as she walked to the front door, then reminded himself that his family was watching him and he turned to finish the job of cleaning the young pup.

Beth hugged the gift to her chest and hurriedly climbed with it up to her room. Thumbelina stretched on her bed, raising a languid paw in greeting. Beth laughed gaily, then hurried to strip off her clothes and wash with the bowl, pitcher, and lavender soap on her dresser. She knew her blueberry dress was beyond repair and thought with regret that she'd have to wear something else.

She shimmied into a light shift, then looked at the few dresses hung on the wall pegs and sighed. Everything looked like what it was—a dress she worked in or wore to take care of the sheep. A rattling noise made her look down at the bed to see Thumbelina scratching at the wrapping of Aenti Ruth's gift.

Beth gently took the package from her friend and opened it with a thrill of excitement. She loved surprise presents and realized that it had been a long while since she'd opened a gift for herself. Her thoughts dwelt briefly on her *fater* and the small surprises he'd often given her. For the first time, the memory didn't cause her pain or shame.

As the wrapping gave way, she stared down at the beautiful fabric inside, then held it up to examine it more closely. It was a simple yet charming dress of lavender material—the sort of light dress that suggested summer breezes and flowers and beauty. And, to her amazement, it seemed as though it was made to her size. She slipped the dress over her head and went to peer in the small looking glass above her dresser. The dress did fit and seemed to cast some pretty enchantment over her mousy hair and blue eyes, but she had little time to wonder how Aenti Ruth had known her size—Ransom was waiting outside with everyone else. She quickly donned a fresh apron and swept Thumbelina close for a brief hug before hurrying back down the loft ladder.

* * *

Ransom turned to the front porch of the Mast cabin when he heard the screen door squeak. He blinked as Beth stepped from the shadows into the light. She looked more beautiful than he'd ever seen her, like a lilac in full bloom. He'd loved the blueberry dress, but this new color was truly something special on her gentle curves.

He stepped closer to her, longing to simply sweep her up in his arms and carry her into the forest to kiss her senseless, but he knew he was being fanciful, so he reached out and took her small hand in his and led her to the wagon. He swung her up and into the hay-filled wagon bed, then quickly joined her and his *mamm* and Aenti Ruth and Abel.

He caught Beth's whispered words of gratitude to Aenti Ruth, then watched the *auld* woman settle back, sure of a job well sewn.

Chapter Thirty-One

Beth helped Ransom's mother arrange some cushions around Aenti Ruth's foot. The *auld* woman was comfortably propped in a large chair in the shade of a great maple—close enough to the frolic to feel a part of the fun. Her animal family clustered close to her and Jack perched on her shoulder.

Beth bent to kiss Aenti Ruth's cheek and whispered softly to her. "*Danki* again for the dress. I appreciate the gift so much."

"Well, see that no one tells you that you look anything but your best in it, dear child. Because you're as pretty as a flower in full bloom."

Beth knew that the *auld* woman was referring to Viola, and Beth realized that such a comment from her *stepmamm* would not hold the power over her that it once had.

Beth nodded. "I promise. Would you like a glass of iced tea?"

"That would be fine, child."

Beth slipped away to the large circular table that held glass gallon jars full of a variety of iced teas—honey mint, lavender sweet, licorice, and several more. She chose the honey mint for Aenti Ruth and was about to make her way back to the maple tree when she heard a male voice quite close to her.

"May I say you look beautiful without offending your Amish belief that vanity is a sin?"

Beth turned and flushed at Ryan Mason's comment. She didn't want his compliments—only Ransom's sweet words—and she straightened her spine.

"*Danki*," she said stiffly.

Ryan suddenly broke into a broad smile. "Ah, so it's worked out God's Way."

She stared at him in surprise. "Wh–what do you mean?"

"Oh, about you and Ransom—and the truth, I would say."

"I don't know how you know," she whispered. "But, *jah*, I think the truth is between us now."

"That's an excellent way to put things, Miss Mast." He lifted a glass of tea from the table near her, then smiled and walked away.

Beth stared after him for a moment, aware that she felt a sense of hard-won peace when the *Englischer* was around, but in no way did it compare with the love she felt for Ransom. *Love . . . It makes me feel like singing . . . like my heart is singing!* She'd never thought she'd have someone in her life to love, someone she wanted to give to and spend time with. . . . All of the words of encouragement Ransom had spoken to her came rushing back into her mind, tumbling over one another like gentle waves of delight.

She handed Aenti Ruth her tea in a dreamy fashion that nearly caused her to step on Pig's cage.

"Ach, I'm terribly sorry, Pig," she apologized, bending to put her finger on the little guinea pig's nose. Aenti Ruth settled once more into her cushions, and

Beth stood by her side, wondering if she should stay until the *auld* woman dozed.

"Run along, child," Aenti Ruth said after a moment. "It's only too soon that you become seventy from seventeen—though I know you're twenty, of course."

Beth bent to impulsively kiss Aenti Ruth's wrinkled cheek and was gently waved away. "*Geh* and have fun, Beth."

"Ach, I will, but I'll *kumme* back to check on you."

Beth turned in time to find Lucy coming gaily over to grab her hand and haul her along to one of the nearby cabins.

The work was done on the outside of the cabin and women were organizing the inside furniture with efficient grace. Lucy pulled her into the large master bedroom, then turned to Beth with sparkling eyes.

"I can see it on your face, Beth Mast. You're glowing!" Lucy dropped her voice when another woman placed a small footstool beside the big, four-poster bed. "You're in love," she whispered.

Beth couldn't contain a quiet laugh of joy as she began to tell Lucy all her friend wanted to know of her feelings for Ransom.

Ransom had to focus for the tenth time on the varnishing he was doing to a nearly finished oak bed. He'd spent the last half hour either looking for Beth or daydreaming about her. He'd never known his thoughts to be so tangled, and when Abel gave him a nudge on the shoulder, he turned in surprise.

"What do you need, little *bruder*?"

"Bishop Umble's looking for you, but you'd better take that look off your face before you meet with him."

"Hmmm?"

Ransom heard his brother give a mock groan as the *buwe* turned away, only to be replaced by the bishop, heartily calling his name.

"Ransom! There you be . . . I'd like to talk with you a bit."

Ransom cleared his throat and laid down the varnish brush carefully. "*Jah*, Bishop? What is it?"

Bishop Umble's blue eyes sparked both with wisdom and an odd touch of amusement. "I'd like to have a talk with you about when you'd like us to start preparing for the wedding. You know, the feast is the biggest part, really, and—"

"Wait? What? Whose wedding?"

Bishop Umble clapped him on the shoulder. "You really are comedic, *sohn*. Whose wedding? Why, yours and dear Beth Mast's."

Ransom swallowed, then found himself nodding in agreement as his heart filled with exhilaration. *A wedding . . . with Beth? We haven't even courted properly, but maybe we could do that after we wed. . . .* His thoughts wrangled round themselves until he finally found the words to speak. "Suppose she won't have me?"

The bishop smiled. "Do you think, *buwe*, that that's any way to trust in Derr Herr . . . and His Truth?"

"*Nee*," Ransom said seriously. "I suppose it's not."

"*Gut!* Then let's *geh* judge the pies with Ryan Mason, who's leaving Ice Mountain tomorrow, by the way. I'd say the *buwe* has gotten about all he can in understanding our people and will make a natural keeper of the Ice Mine shop. And I've tried to help him as much as I can with his life in student ministry."

"But tomorrow? I didn't expect that he'd *geh* straight off. . . ."

"You've grown to appreciate the *Englischer, jah*?"

"He's given me a great gift," Ransom said slowly, meeting the bishop's kind eyes. "I need to thank him."

"Then do that, *sohn*. Right after we judge the pies and right after you ask Beth to marry you."

"Right . . . right after."

Beth had helped paint the walls of one of the cabins' kitchens a tempered light blue, then she'd moved on to place bright red geraniums in coffee cans on the windowsills. The smell of fresh wood shavings and the general bustle of activity that hummed around her made her feel happy and she couldn't help looking here and there for Ransom as she worked.

She hadn't seen Viola, for which she was thankful, and she'd received many an approving glance from the women of the community. She was just ready to dust the benches of a large table when one of Olivia Lott's young *dochders* came and asked her if she would pick flowers with her to help decorate the *dollhaus* that she and Ransom had given to the Lotts that morning. Olivia had cried in gratitude while the children were ecstatic—making all the work on the toy more than worthwhile.

Now, Beth decided that occupying the little *maedel* with flower hunting a bit would be both helpful and fun, so she took the child's hand and set off with her into the nearby woods to find wildflowers. Soon, they had collected delicate blossoms of pink and yellow, light blue and white Queen Anne's lace. They were making their way deeper into the forest, following the lure of some lady's slipper when Beth suddenly caught the child's hand as a chill went down her spine. She might have been mistaken at the noise, but then it came again, and Beth cast worried eyes over the forest floor. The little girl broke from her grasp to grab at the bright yellow flower when Beth saw a large timber rattler coiled in strike position. She pulled the child to safety only to feel the primeval and painful bite of the snake on her arm. . . .

Chapter Thirty-Two

Ransom took a bite of the neatly sliced peach pie and decided it was a shade too dry when he mentally compared it to Beth's pies, but he kept smiling and moved on to the next in the fine array of desserts the women of Ice Mountain had created. He, Bishop Umble, and Ryan Mason were the judges of the day, and Ransom traded good-natured remarks with the crowd as well as his fellow judges. He came next to a rather too-browned pie with a sadly shaped dough heart in the middle and something went off in his mind that he felt he should remember about this particular pie, but it eluded him. He lifted the pie a bit, intent on giving it a fair chance when the hum of conversation was broken by a child's piercing screams.

Ransom recognized the young daughter of Olivia Lott and felt a strange dread overtake him. He scanned the people gathered but didn't see a lavender dress like Beth's. He put down the pie without looking at the table and absently heard it fall to the ground with a dull thud. Then he moved through the crowd and knelt by the sobbing little *maedel* as she wailed in her mother's arms.

"It's Beth, Ransom," Olivia Lott said worriedly.

"I saw them go off into the woods about half an hour ago."

Ransom got to his feet and patted her shoulder. "It'll be fine," he muttered, then headed for the forest, still unsure of what he would find. . . .

Beth watched the large rattler slither off into a den of nearby rocks. Once the snake was gone, she got to her knees and then lay down on the ground, the bite on her arm burning terribly. She stared up at the blue sky, visible between the tall trees, and tried to slow her breathing. She knew that the more frightened she became, the more quickly the venom would go to her heart. She prayed as the moments slipped by, wondering if she were to die without sharing with Ransom how very much she loved him. Her mind drifted as she felt her pulse begin to thrum in her ears and then faintly, as if on the edge of a dream, she heard Ransom roar her name. . . .

Ransom saw Beth lying on the light brown pine needles of the forest floor and rushed to her side. She looked pale, and he immediately slid his fingers to her throat to feel her pulse. She was muttering and he caught the word "snake," and then he began to search her arms and legs for the bite mark he knew would be there. He saw the reddish puncture wounds on her right inner arm, just above her wrist, and saw the diameter of the bite marks. *It was a big snake.* . . . He was suddenly battling the same emotions he'd felt when Barbara was in the car crash and he'd been helpless to do anything. . . . *But not now, not this time . . .* He reached in his pocket for the small knife he always carried and began to pray.

With quick and careful strokes, he cut an "X" between and across the puncture marks and bent his head to suck the poison from the wound. He vaguely registered that she whimpered and he increased the draw of his mouth. . . .

It's all right, little hare. . . . It's all right. Gott *is with us and you're going to be fine. Dear* Gott, *let her live . . .*

He realized that someone touched his shoulder and heard a calm female voice from far away.

"Ransom." It was Sarah Mast, the healer. "Stop now. You know you're endangering your own life . . . *Sei se gut,* carry Beth back to my cabin. I have antivenom."

He heard his own choked sob as he stopped abruptly, then swept Beth up into his arms and carried her easily from the shadows of the forest.

Beth was aware of the strangest sensations as she struggled through the fog in her mind that seemed to have no end. She felt cocooned in warmth but then was too hot, only to feel herself shake with chills that seemed to penetrate to her very bones. She thought she heard Viola call her name and struggled to respond, but then it didn't seem important. She was looking for Ransom, desperate to get to him—but Ice Mountain was living up to its name and snow fell with a swirling force, creating steep hills that were too slippery for her to tread in her summer bare feet. Her arm burned terribly and she turned her head to see her daed *standing beside her. He seemed a wonder and was smiling in translucent light. She wondered if she might* geh *to him—just for a moment. . . .*

* * *

"How many vials has that been?" Ransom asked
Sarah in a low voice. He couldn't take his eyes away
from the sight of Beth, lying flushed and feverish in
the healer's bed.

"Five. I'm fortunate to have it on hand, though I
think my herbal mixture is helping as well."

"*Jah*," Ransom whispered. "Pray *Gott* that it is."

He reached down to run a finger across Beth's
cheek, wanting to see her beautiful eyes open and
clear, her gentle smile, and to hear her soft words—
balm to his heart.

"Ransom—Viola is waiting in the other room,"
Sarah murmured. "She asks to see Beth."

"She asks," he said bitterly. "A first, I'm sure."

"Anger will not help Beth," Sarah said firmly. "I'll
tell Viola to *kumme* in."

He moved around to the far side of the bed, his
arm braced against the log wall, but not even its stur-
diness seemed real to him.

Viola entered stiffly, looking first at him, then
averting her gaze to study Beth. The *aulder* woman
cleared her throat. "She—she looks asleep."

"It's the fever."

"*Jah*, of course." Viola's voice cracked a bit, and
Ransom gave her a speculative look.

"Do you pretend to care?"

"Of course I care." Viola glared at him. "She is my
stepdochder."

Yeah, and your servant too. . . . He wanted to say it
but couldn't bring himself to speak such negative
words over Beth while her life hung in the balance.

He watched Viola reach down to stroke one of

Beth's small hands. "My first husband . . . he . . . we had a *dochder* much like Beth. The child died from the grippe, hours after she'd taken ill. I always thought *Gott* gave back by allowing me to parent one such as Beth, but after her *fater* died . . . I . . . it seemed easier to lean on Beth than to think about how she might feel."

Ransom sighed. He knew that such an admission was unlike Viola, but if he intended to marry Beth, he must find a way to honor Viola as well. But he was saved from giving a proper response when Beth stirred and opened her blue eyes, blinking up at him in owl-like fashion.

"I saw my *fater*."

Ransom shook his head, feeling tears burn his eyes as he leaned close. "But now you're here, sweet Beth. Here with me."

He bent to kiss her brow and heard her soft whisper. "I love you, Ransom. I love you."

Chapter Thirty-Three

Beth's recovery was slow and she chafed at the delay. But her arm was healing and Sarah had told her that Ransom's decision to suck out the venom had been key to her survival.

Now she sat, strangely ensconced in Viola's comfortable bed while her *stepmamm* had slept on the couch for the past nights and willingly brought Beth tea and iced limeade to drink. Beth had initially been bewildered by the change in Viola's manner toward her, but her *stepmamm* had told her one evening that she'd been wrong. Beth still recalled the scene of that conversation as though looking through a cloudy glass. Viola had offered her iced tea, then pulled a chair close to the bed.

"Beth, I find that—in nearly losing you—I have been remiss in the way that I have treated you these many years since your *fater*'s death."

"Uh . . . Viola. *Danki*, but you don't have to . . . I mean . . ." She'd stopped in confusion, not wanting to turn aside the only words of peace Viola had offered her in years.

Her *stepmamm* had leaned close and Beth saw the

tears that filled the faded green eyes. "*Nee*, Beth . . . *sei se gut* . . . hear what I say."

Beth had nodded, and when Viola extended both her aged hands to her, Beth had taken them with feelings of thankfulness and joy.

"Well, I suppose I hate to say it, but I'll miss you." Ransom spoke the words with a smile as he extended a hand to Ryan Mason.

The *Englischer* adjusted his knapsack on his back and grinned as he accepted the handshake. "You know I'm only as far away as Coudersport, friend . . . and I'll have the ice cream and gift shop up and running at the Ice Mine next spring. I'm glad everything's worked out so well for you and Beth."

"As to that, I owe you deep thanks and I'm extending an official invitation to our wedding, come this September."

"You've asked her?"

Ransom gave him a sour look. "Put away the mind reading, Mason. *Nee*, I'm going to ask her tonight."

"Ahhh."

"Don't tell me. I don't want to know how she'll answer."

Ryan lifted a hand in farewell as he turned and started down the faint path through the tall timber. "Don't worry, Ransom—you're sure to take it like a man!"

"*Danki!*"

Ransom smiled at the youth pastor's words but then drew a deep breath. *What will Beth say? Perhaps it's all too soon . . .* But then he remembered their kisses and decided that soon might not be soon enough.

Rose and Viola had gone to bed, and Beth sat in the coolness of the *nacht* on the front porch rocking chair. She wore a light robe over a cotton shift and no shoes. Lightning bugs danced in fine array to some silent orchestral arrangement and she smiled at the summer beauty. But she could feel a slight chill in the air, a portent that autumn would soon come to Ice Mountain—a time for harvest and canning and pumpkins and snuggling under patchwork quilts at the end of the day.

She shivered, wondering what it might be like to bundle with Ransom, an intimate part of courting. Couples would share a bed with a bundling board set between them. Then they might talk or kiss, but nothing further might be done. Beth imagined, though, that Ransom would find a way to express his feelings for her and delighted in the thought.

"What are you thinking of, sweetheart?"

Beth nearly jumped out of her chair. "Ransom! You scared me to death!"

She felt him sit down at her feet in the faint light of the moon.

"Did I, now? But you still haven't answered my question."

Beth cleared her throat and was glad when her voice came out light and airy. "I was—admiring the lightning bugs. That's all."

Ransom pressed his shoulder against her knees

and leaned in to rub his big hands tenderly up her legs. "I don't believe you, little hare."

"Why . . . not?" She swallowed against the warm wash of sensation his touch provoked.

"Because I can tell your breathing is a little too fast and I think you looked, shall we say, wistful, in the light of the moon."

"Mmm . . . perhaps," she admitted finally as she closed her eyes for a moment, imagining what it would be like to have him touch her thighs, but then he drew away abruptly. She was startled, then realized that he had only moved to change position and now knelt in front of her. Her hands reached out and felt the smooth brush of his hair, then traced his face, moving over brows and high cheekbones, the outline of his firm mouth. He turned his lips into the palm of her hand and she shivered in delight as the tip of his tongue teased her tender flesh.

He pulled away after a moment, though, and she fancied she could see the dark gleam of his eyes in the moonlight.

"Ach, sweet Beth . . . marry me, *sei se gut*," he whispered, and she felt her heart leap with sudden joy. "Marry me."

Whatever he'd planned on saying had been lost in a quick flood of emotion once he'd started to kiss her. Yet the words he spoke rang with truth in his heart. He paused, breathless, and waited in the shadows for her response.

"Ach, Ransom. *Jah. Jah*, I'll marry you." She melted

into his arms and he sank back on his haunches and lifted her from the chair into his lap.

"Ach, Beth . . . You're so soft and wonderful. I want . . . I think . . ."

"Don't think, Ransom."

He blinked at her words. She sounded confident and assured, so much more a woman than a girl, and he fell to kissing her once more.

Chapter Thirty-Four

Beth soon realized that although most of Ice Mountain was excited and happy for Ransom and herself, there was one person who most definitely was not. Her stepsister, Rose, held herself aloof from any overtures of kindness Beth tried to make, and even went so far as to ignore Viola's changed attitude toward Beth.

Beth thought she understood—surely Rose was upset because she'd loved Ransom herself. She'd even said as much at breakfast when Beth had rather shyly announced her intention to marry Ransom.

"Marry? Ridiculous! Why, he's making a *gut* joke of you, Beth! I'm surprised you took him seriously."

Beth prayed to herself as she buttered a slice of toast. Finally, she spoke, her voice even and controlled. "Rose, you are beautiful and I've *kumme* to know that I—I am as well. *Gott* will surely bring you love in your life, perhaps sooner than—"

"Mamm," Rose wailed. "Do you hear how she speaks to me? Make her stop!"

Beth was truly surprised when Viola gently told Rose to either be polite or leave the table.

"I am not going to have Beth stop, Rose," Viola

continued. "She has a right to speak. And I must say that if she is to be married, we will do our best to celebrate with a wedding feast unlike any other!"

Beth saw the stormy expression that marred her stepsister's lovely face and just missed being splattered by hot coffee when Rose threw the remains of her cup and left the table in a high rage.

Viola cleared her throat as she reached to dab at the coffee with her cloth napkin. "I've spoiled the child. It's my doing, but perhaps she will *kumme* to change her mind as time goes on."

Beth nodded her assent but was deeply doubtful.

The days passed and Ice Mountain bid a fond farewell to Olivia Lott and her children. Ransom happened to be at the cabins when the *Englischwoman* was leaving and was surprised when she gave him a quick *buss* on the cheek. "Thank you, Ransom, for thinking of these cabins of rest. It's made a huge difference in our lives. We've been able to heal here in a way we never could have in that other world. But we're ready to go back. School and everything, you know."

"We'll all miss you."

Olivia smiled. "That reminds me. . . . I have something for Beth. Please give it to her for me."

Ransom accepted the small white box with pleasure. "I surely will."

Olivia nodded her thanks, then turned to leave with the party of men and women who were escorting her down the mountain, while Ransom went back to collect the chisel he'd accidentally left at the cabins.

He found the tool and was about to leave the bright and airy front room when the cabin door eased open. He turned with a ready greeting on his lips only to frown as Rose slipped inside. He didn't like the crafty smile she wore and he moved to brush past her, but she put a hand on his chest.

"Ach, Ransom, where are you going? I thought we might have some private time together to discuss our future."

He looked down at her warily, not wanting to hurt one of Beth's family but having no desire to give Rose any ideas.

"I'm on my way back to the mill, Rose," he said politely. "What is it you want to say?"

She slipped her arms up around his shoulders and blinked at him with a simpering look. "I know it's foolishness what Beth says about marrying you. I know it's me that you want." She stood on tiptoe in an obvious bid to kiss him, but he put her from him and shook his head.

"Rose, you must believe what I say—I love Beth."

Her mouth curved in a sneer. "How could you love her? She's fat! You are simply being kind."

A rush of anger surged through him. "*Gott* hears your words," he finally bit out. "And I must go." He walked away from her, his back turned, but he heard her scream nonetheless.

"Fair enough, Ransom King! But there will be no wedding—mark my words!"

He blew out a breath of exasperation and kept walking, but some niggle of fear touched him before he dismissed it and went whistling back to the mill.

* * *

Petunia let out a sonorous snore and Aenti Ruth gently nudged the pig with her toe.

"All right, Petunia, we're ready to set out."

Beth giggled as the pig snorted to awareness. The rest of the animal family was gathered about as Aenti Ruth got to her feet. Her ankle was wrapped sturdily, and Sarah had pronounced it fit for walking with a stick, so long as the *auld* woman didn't overdo.

But today, Aenti Ruth had insisted that she and Beth walk the short distance to Ben Kauffman's store to purchase the fabric for Beth's wedding dress.

"It's my gift to you, child, and I'll take pleasure in helping you make it up, if you'll permit an *auld* woman's sewing?"

Beth smiled as she managed the leashes of the pups while Jack balanced on her shoulder. "I'd love it, and I know it would be a help to Viola. . . . She's insisting that I have a wedding quilting and the preparations are huge. I told her it really wasn't necessary."

"Your *stepmamm* is quite right," Aenti Ruth said with a nod of her silver head. "You deserve a wedding with all of the celebration."

Beth laughed a bit in appreciation. "I still can't quite believe it. . . ." *Though Ransom's heated kisses tell me the truth of the matter . . .*

"Well, believe it, child. It will be my true joy to welcome you into the family and, of course, your *kinner* in due time."

Beth couldn't contain the blush she knew stained her cheeks, and Aenti Ruth chortled. "That's the blush of an innocent maid, and I'll say no more as we're here."

Aenti Ruth managed the stairs with a minimum of fuss while Beth held open the big wooden door. They were greeted by a shower of good wishes that were as fragrant to Beth's soul as the rich aroma of the store was to the senses. It was not often that an upcoming wedding was spoken about so openly, but with Beth's recovery from the snakebite, there was extra reason for celebration.

"*Gott* bless you and Ransom both." Beth received the embrace of an older girl with a smile, then tried to wrangle the pups through the busy store. When she and Aenti Ruth reached the back counter, Ben Kauffman himself came forward to wait on them.

"Now then, Beth Mast, what is it I might do for you?"

Beth was saved from replying when Aenti Ruth tapped on the gregarious store owner's hand with the top of her walking stick. "Now, Benjamin, there'll be no teasing of the *maedel*. It's wedding dress fabric she wants and you know it well."

Beth wanted to crawl under the counter but focused instead on the array of blue fabric that was promptly presented for inspection. She drew a deep breath and decided to enjoy the moment. "This one, I think." She smiled.

"An excellent choice, my child," Aenti Ruth approved. "It matches the blue of your eyes perfectly. Wrap it up, Benjamin, and I'll be the one paying."

"Ach, *nee*, Aenti Ruth. Viola has given me money and I've barely used any of it."

"It's my gift for the wedding."

"*Danki*," Beth whispered and bent close to kiss her wrinkled cheek.

* * *

Ransom slipped from the cabin into the dark and walked the distance to the Mast cabin. He didn't want to bother Beth with the encounter he'd had with Rose that morning and was glad to see that only one lamp burned in the kitchen as he approached.

Beth sat, diligently sewing, the warmth of the light shining about her, and he felt his heart begin to pound in anticipation of touching her. He tapped lightly on the window and she looked up with a warm smile on her lips as she rose to let him in.

"Ach, little hare, you feel so *gut*," he muttered as he pulled her close, letting his lips find the secret spot behind her shell-like ear that always made her shiver in delight.

But his body became more insistent and he finally pulled away with true regret. She gave him a delightful pout and he bent to whisper against her neck. "I think Viola would prefer not to have a pregnant bride." He laughed when she slapped his upper arms in feigned anger.

"But perhaps I would prefer it," she said softly, and he blinked in surprise.

"You never stop amazing me, sweet Beth. Now tell me what you are sewing with such diligence."

She gave a sudden squeak and tried to turn him from the table, but he spun back around.

"Is it a surprise?"

"It's my wedding dress, and I don't think you should see it."

"Whyever not?" he asked with a raised brow. "I think the superstition goes that I shouldn't see you in it before our wedding day. Seeing it sitting on the table is perfectly innocent."

He smiled as she considered. "Okay. I suppose you're right."

She led him to the kitchen table and he snuggled close to her as she slid in on the bench. He watched her small hands smooth the sky-blue fabric, then continued with her work. She handled the thread with precision and glanced up at him once with an obviously shy expression. He slid closer and wrapped an arm around the sweet curve of her lower back.

"I–I'm just basting, you know. . . . Your Aenti Ruth wants to help on the, um, final sewing. . . ." Her voice came out in a confused whisper, as if she were having trouble concentrating.

"Go on," he said softly, though his hand tingled and his heart pounded as he moved even closer to her.

She turned and looked at him helplessly. "Ransom—I . . ."

He kissed her slowly, as if he was savoring some warm, melting sweet, and she responded with tentative touches of her tongue to his. It took everything he had to control himself. He pulled away with abrupt force and got to his feet.

"What's wrong?" Her lips were cherry red and slightly swollen, and he groaned aloud.

"Nothing's wrong. I just think I need a bath."

"A bath?"

He ignored her doubtful look. "*Jah.* In the creek."

He left the room and was out the cabin door before she could reply.

Chapter Thirty-Five

The days passed and August's heat gave way to the crimson shine of September as preparations for the wedding took on a fever pitch. A large quilting frame had been borrowed from the Loftus family and set up in the front room of the Mast cabin. And once wooden benches were added to all sides, there was barely enough room to walk around it, yet Aenti Ruth had agreed to leave only the dogs at home. Consequently, Petunia took up sprawling residence on the couch, next to Pig, and Jack cavorted about, scaring some of the more timid women present.

The quilt squares had been pieced together by Lucy, Mary Lyons, and Priscilla King, as well as some of the older girls from Jude Lyons's class. Beth was truly amazed when she surveyed the wide quilt top stretched out on the wooden frame. Women had sent over quilt squares of intricate design and beauty. There was a chestnut tree near a bubbling stream, a rainbow at sunset, a squirrel playing in a pile of leaves, a detailed outline of Ice Mountain itself, and many more designs. Beth was amazed and thankful for each woman's contribution as she surveyed the pristine top. Then she noticed a large pink pig halfway across the top, and as she peered closer, she realized it was surely a square from Aenti Ruth.

Beth skirted round the table to *buss* the *auld* woman's cheek, then went about being hugged and kissed by those gathered until she took her place of honor at the head of the frame. She pulled needle and thread to her and rejoiced in the homey sounds of the women talking gently, the clink of teacups from the kitchen—for Viola had insisted, along with several other women, on preparing the snacks for the quilting, as well as the tea.

As Beth sewed, she thought of Rose. Her stepsister has been acting a bit odd of late—frequently screaming at Beth but then becoming sullen and silent. And she wasn't present at the quilting today. Beth sighed but then refocused on the bounty surrounding her. *Gott* had changed her life with His love and with the freedom that comes from telling the truth. Now that Ransom had *kumme* into her life, she felt loved and held and wonderful.

Just then, as if on cue, there was a brisk knock at the front door. Viola bustled to get it and came back carrying a beautiful cherrywood quilt stand emblazoned with a bright blue ribbon.

"Beth, I think you have a gift." Viola smiled and handed Beth the card that was attached.

Beth felt herself flush as she accepted the folded paper. She flushed even more when she read Ransom's note, written in bold print. "To my *maedel*, I look forward to enjoying all of life's celebrations with you. Have a *gut* time! I love you, Ransom."

After that, the morning flew by in a round of pleasant chatter and quilting. Little *maedels* loved to run beneath the raised quilt frame and retrieve dropped needles, and everyone enjoyed lingering in the kitchen and outdoor porch to sample the hot tea, fresh cucumber and tomato and cheese finger sandwiches, as well as the black walnut cookies dusted with powdered sugar.

It was only when they had regained their places around the quilt frame that they began to discuss what they were bringing to the wedding feast in a week's time.

While the women gathered to quilt, most of the men of Ice Mountain took it upon themselves to gather at Ben Kauffman's store to play a checkers tournament and to share in a celebratory sip of white lightning. Ben also served smoked cheese, venison bologna, and horseradish with crackers to tempt the appetite.

After teasing Ransom for a *gut* while about his upcoming marriage, the men fell to nostalgia and to telling stories about the women in their own lives.

Jude Lyons spoke with a smile about the shotgun wedding he'd had. "In truth, it was the best day of my life." The former *Englischer* laughed.

"Mine too," Edward King chimed in. "Seems like in our family, only Joe here, got to pick his pretty miss."

"*Danki.*" Joseph smiled. "She is more than pretty, though, younger *bruder.*"

Ransom grinned, enjoying the camaraderie of the men. He realized that he was accepted, and the feeling matched the love he had in his heart for Beth—the kind of feeling that ran through the cracks of the past and made them whole again.

"How about any advice on marriage—" he ventured during a lull in the conversation.

Henry Loftus chortled. "Now, *buwe*, remember that the *gut* Bishop Umble is present."

Ransom saw the bishop look up from the checkerboard with a gleam in his bright blue eyes. "I could tell you to always be the man of the house, but somehow, I think that Martha would have my head. So, I'll tell you instead, Ransom, that never should you feel that you are the stronger one in the marriage. . . . *Nee*, women are tempered like fine steel and can bend but not break. They bear hardship and children—"

Ransom, as well as the rest of Ice Mountain, knew the *auld* man paused because Martha had suffered many miscarriages. He felt his throat tighten when he thought of the child he had lost with Barbara. . . .

"But . . ." Bishop Umble went on, "the Lord gives back. He is faithful. Now king me, Mahlon Mast!"

The air of joviality returned and Ransom gathered many more succinct ideas on marriage.

As Beth wearily washed the last of the dishes from the quilting, Viola told her to *geh* to bed. "I'll finish here, Beth. Though I wish Rose had *kumme* today. I don't know what to make of the child lately."

Beth frowned, feeling unaccountably troubled about her stepsister. "I know. I didn't see her the whole day."

Viola nodded. "She's probably in her room. I'll check in on her when I'm through here."

"Ach, Viola, let me, *sei se gut* . . . I'd like to talk to Rose about how she's been feeling lately."

"*Jah*, that would be kind of you."

Beth smiled and turned to go to the loft ladder. She realized as she climbed that the moon was full and gave an illuminated enchantment to her room. She tiredly turned up the lamp and nearly jumped when she realized that Rose was sitting on her bed, holding a large pair of sewing shears.

"Rose?"

Rose got to her feet. "Hello, favored daughter. How do you feel as you prepare for a wedding that will never happen?"

"Rose, you're not yourself."

"I am very much myself." Her hand stroked the shears. "Very, very much."

Beth followed her stepsister's gaze across the small, slanted room, where her wedding dress hung neatly on a peg. But there was something wrong with it—the material seemed almost billowy in the breeze from the window.

"That's right, little stepsister. Your wedding dress. What a shame it needed alteration." Rose laughed lightly and turned up the lamp.

Beth watched as her wedding dress was illuminated; the hopelessly shredded blue material hung in slashed ribbons.

"Rose, what have you done?" Beth whispered.

"Ask me what I'm going to do, little Beth . . . that's the more important question. . . ."

Chapter Thirty-Six

Ransom had had a bit too much to drink and was dreaming of Beth as he made his way through the dark woods, knowing the paths by heart. He was headed for the Mast cabin to do some late-night courting when he saw the light of a single lantern bobbing unsteadily through the woods ahead of him.

"Hullo," he called, expecting that it was someone else having a late-*nacht* wander.

"Ransom! Don't—"

He recognized Beth's cry, and fear ran down his spine, sobering him with instant force. "Beth? Are you all right?"

"She's just fine, Ransom. Aren't you, Beth?"

The lantern was probably ten feet away and Ransom recognized that Rose was prodding Beth with something that flashed silver in the light. "Rose?" Some instinct made him keep his voice low and steady, as if soothing a wild creature. "Rose, what's going on?"

"I'm eliminating our problem, Ransom." Rose lifted the lantern, and Ransom took the scene in with one horrified look.

Beth wore a slashed blue dress, and blood from

several cuts ran red over the fabric. Her hair was loose and the sewing shears in Rose's hand flashed with cruel intent at her side.

"Rose—you–you think we are to marry, you and I?"

He heard the girl catch her breath, almost in a sob. "*Jah*, Ransom. That's all I really want."

"*Gut.* Then let me get close to you and we can both . . . eliminate . . . the problem."

Rose laughed, an eerie sound, as she raised the light higher. "Do you hear, you stupid, silly cow? It's me who he wants. Not you. Never you."

Ransom was fast, but Beth was faster. She turned to face Rose, wresting the shears from her stepsister's hand and giving the other girl a hard push so that she dropped the lantern and staggered backward.

"It's over, Rose," Beth said clearly. "And I am no cow nor coward either. You chose poorly."

Ransom felt a surge of pride at Beth's keen words. He caught her to him, putting an arm around her and touching her now-shaking hands. "I'm proud of you, sweetheart," he whispered into the wild mass of her hair. He lifted the lantern and saw Beth's tremulous smile, then bent to kiss her once before turning to where Rose sat on the forest floor.

Rose was sobbing and looked bewildered in the lantern's light. "Beth, Ransom . . . ach, what have I done? What have I done?"

Ransom was surprised when Beth left his arms to *geh* and comfort her stepsister. "It's all right, Rose. I think you're sick and need some help—that's all."

Ransom watched Rose nod slowly. "I cut you; I'm so sorry."

"Nothing too bad—now let's get you home. You're shaking like a leaf."

"Beth, I stole your recipe card from that secret place in your dresser."

"I know." Ransom heard Beth speak tenderly, as if to a child. "But I remember the recipe, Rose. So, there's no harm done. *Kumme*, let's get out of the *nacht* before you take a chill."

Beth glanced up at Ransom and saw the silent plea in her eyes. He handed her the lantern, then gently lifted Rose into his arms and led the way home.

Beth listened carefully to Viola as she spoke over the telephone that Sebastian Christener was allowed to keep in his workshop. Several members of the community and the bishop had helped Rose and Viola down the mountain to the *Englischer's haus* at the bottom. Mr. Ellis had driven them to Lancaster, where there was a mental health facility.

Rose was going to stay there until she was well and Viola promised to be back in a few days. Viola said Rose was suffering from depression and an anxiety disorder and needed medicines to help her, as well as talking to one of the doctors there on a regular basis. She would probably *kumme* home in a few weeks.

Beth hung up the phone and nodded a shy thank-you to Sebastian before being swept into Ransom's arms.

"You're coming home with me, sweet Beth, and you're going to sleep the day away."

"But—the wedding, Ransom! And the food for the feast! Why, I've got to . . ."

She stopped as he gave her a lingering kiss. "Sleep first, okay?"

Beth smiled. "Okay."

When she was safely ensconced in the Kings' master bedroom, Ransom came in to kneel beside the bed. "Are you all right, little hare? When I think of what might have happened . . ."

She reached up to touch his cheek with tenderness.

"*Gott* kept me safe, Ransom. Truly."

"Mmm." He lightly stroked her lips. "I wondered about the card Rose said she had stolen from you. A recipe card?"

"Your Aenti Ruth gave it to me one day. It was 'A Recipe for Loving Yourself.'"

"And you memorized it?"

"Mmm-hmmm." She leaned sideways to kiss him. "But I can't tell you unless Aenti Ruth gives her permission."

Ransom rolled his eyes even as they kissed. "Like that's going to happen."

Beth smiled as she bit his lip lightly. "You never know, Ransom. You never know."

Chapter Thirty-Seven

A wedding on Ice Mountain was cause for celebration, and everyone came together to help. Next
to the service, the wedding feast itself was meant to
display the abundance of *Gott*'s love and the love the
couple shared with each other and the community.

"This is nerve-racking," Ransom muttered as Jeb
helped him with his tie and long black coat.

Jeb laughed. "Wait 'til your wedding night."

"Some help you are, big *bruder*," Ransom said ruefully. "I didn't realize I'd feel like all eyes are on me."

"Well, some are on the bride too, you know!"

"Right." Ransom grinned, already having stolen
some early morning kisses from Beth by jogging to
the Mast *haus* and back again.

The two *bruders* went into the kitchen, and Ransom
eyed Jeb as he ate with gusto. "You make me sick—
literally," Ransom growled.

Jeb waved a fork at him. "You can eat this afternoon."

"Yeah, like I'm going to want to!"

He decided to wander outside, finding the house
a bit claustrophobic with all the benches and chairs
gathered inside. Viola had consented to the groom's

family hosting the wedding service as she was only just back from seeing Rose, who was doing quite a bit better.

Horses and buggies soon lined the dirt road, and both men and women hailed him with blessings and *gut* wishes.

The time seemed to melt as if sand through his hands, and soon he was sitting in a straight-backed chair with Beth across the aisle from him while Jeb and Lucy acted as attendants. Bishop Umble spoke long and pleasantly while Ransom watched Beth, half-wondering if she'd pass out again. She must have caught his gaze because she smiled, and he loved the delicate curve of her cheek. *We'll have little* maedels . . . *as many as I can carry . . . all looking like her. . . .*

Bishop Umble cleared his throat and Ransom snapped back to attention. Soon it was over, and he took Beth's arm to lead her to the back of the living room, where the wildflower-adorned *eck* had been set up.

He bent to whisper softly in her ear and was pleased with her smile and blush. "Tell me, Miss, or should I say Frau King, would it do if we saved a bit of blueberry pie for our wedding night?"

"Wh–why?"

"Oh, nutrition, and the fact that we might—taste that pie together. Blueberry kisses . . . you know."

"That sounds delightful."

They sat down together behind the table and enjoyed the feeling of being waited on. Then Bishop Umble stood up and the community grew silent. He held a glass of strawberry punch in his aged hand, and Ransom and Beth took up their glasses in unison.

The bishop cleared his throat. "To Ransom and Beth. May Derr Herr bless your union with strength and joy, laughter and *kinner*. And to all of you who love Ice Mountain and have found *Gott* in this blessed place, *kumme* here often and stay for as long as you need."

Epilogue

"Recipe for Loving Yourself"

If it's you, you want to love
Then carry forth with *Gott* above
Not a blot, nor single mar
Can change the worth of who you are
And make the Truth your dearest friend
To satisfy the deepest end. . . .

Please read on for a peek at

Marrying Matthew,

Book One of *The Amish Mail Order Groom* Series
by Kelly Long.

Blackberry Falls, PA

Wanted: An Amish Mail Order Groom. Aged 20–35. Must be willing to live in remote Appalachia and build life in said community. Must love books, horses, and possess good teeth. Appearance must be tolerable, at least, though bride would favor a *gut* mind over looks. Must understand a woman's sensibilities and not be judgmental. Must realize that *Gott* is the Third in a marriage. Reply to . . .

Twenty-year-old Tabitha Stolfus knew that she was both the sole heir of her *fater*'s company and his sole lament.

"If only you'd been born a *buwe*," he'd wail at times. "Or if only you'd marry! Why can't you marry, Tabby? And why must you be so headstrong?"

Tabitha had heard the words so often, she could almost put them to song. But she had finally had enough, so she'd taken out an ad in the *Renova*

Record, a small *Englisch* and Amish newspaper far
from her home in the Allegheny Mountains.

If I'm to have a husband, she'd considered, *let it be
some man who isn't so familiar with the wealth represented
by Stolfus Lumber and Woodworking. This way, I can
make sure he meets the qualifications that I lay out—not
my* fater's.

The idea she'd whispered to herself took root in
her mind and grew, and soon a detailed ad was sub-
mitted to the far-off *Record*. And, to her surprise, an
Amish man responded . . . rather coolly, she thought,
but nonetheless a response.

She'd kept the letter in the bosom of her shift beneath her careful collar and occasionally pulled it
out to read and read again, trying hard to spot anything suspicious that might lie within the words. But
even she had to admit that Matthew King sounded
much to her liking. He didn't seem to know about
Stolfus Lumber and Woodworking and he didn't
seem to possess the ardor common to some of the
local men who'd tried to win her hand . . . and her
purse. *Jah*, Matthew King would do just fine. . . .

"Have you lost your mind, big *bruder*?"

Matthew King shot his younger sibling, Caleb, a
wry glance and then resumed packing. "I've told
you—her da runs one of the best woodworking out-
fits in the mountains."

Caleb snorted. "Then *geh* and ask to apprentice
with him. You don't need to do something *narrisch*
like marrying his headstrong *dochder*. I've heard she's
as wild as a colt and not exactly marriage material."

"It doesn't matter. I want to learn what only her

fater can teach me, and he doesn't favor taking on apprentices. Marrying the girl is incidental. . . ."

Matthew recalled his words with a faint lift of his firm lips, then swiped his arm across his wet face for about the tenth time that morning. It had been raining steadily since he'd left home two days before, and as he and his hulking guide made their way deeper into the Allegheny Mountains, Matthew wondered idly if Blackberry Falls was simply a myth. However, there was nothing mythical about the big-boned Amishman in front of him. Abner, as he'd introduced himself, thrusting out a massive paw of a hand, had spoken simply.

"I'm Abner. Right-hand man of Herr Stolfus. His *dochder* has been like my own since she was but a child."

Matthew had nodded, sensing that there was a test somewhere in the *aulder* man's words, so he kept silent.

Abner grunted after a moment, then growled over the cadence of the rain. "I don't hold with what the *maedel* is doing, marrying blind, and an outsider at that. But I guard her secrets well, so keep that in yer head, *buwe*, for I'll not see her harmed in any way."

Matthew realized that it would be of little use to say that he'd never harmed a woman in his life. He could only imagine what rabbit trails such a comment would produce in *auld* Abner's mind, so once more, he remained quiet.

"Ya don't have much to say fer yerself, *buwe*. Still water may run deep, but Blackberry Falls will not easily welcome a stranger, no matter who he's *kumme* to marry."

Matthew didn't respond; he was distracted by a stand of virgin cherrywood near the muddy trail. He put out a hand and touched the bark of the nearest tree with something akin to a caress.

Abner grunted in obviously reluctant approval. "Well, ya touch the tree like ya would a woman, so perhaps ya ain't so strange."

Matthew smiled, careless of the other man's dire attitude. *Here was virgin timber, and there would be men who knew how best to work it.* His arrangement with Tabitha Stolfus would suit him just fine, he decided as he turned his face upward into the rain, and thanked *Gott* for bringing him to Blackberry Falls. . . .

Books by Bestselling Author
Fern Michaels

___ **The Jury**	0-8217-7878-1	$6.99US/$9.99CAN
___ **Sweet Revenge**	0-8217-7879-X	$6.99US/$9.99CAN
___ **Lethal Justice**	0-8217-7880-3	$6.99US/$9.99CAN
___ **Free Fall**	0-8217-7881-1	$6.99US/$9.99CAN
___ **Fool Me Once**	0-8217-8071-9	$7.99US/$10.99CAN
___ **Vegas Rich**	0-8217-8112-X	$7.99US/$10.99CAN
___ **Hide and Seek**	1-4201-0184-6	$6.99US/$9.99CAN
___ **Hokus Pokus**	1-4201-0185-4	$6.99US/$9.99CAN
___ **Fast Track**	1-4201-0186-2	$6.99US/$9.99CAN
___ **Collateral Damage**	1-4201-0187-0	$6.99US/$9.99CAN
___ **Final Justice**	1-4201-0188-9	$6.99US/$9.99CAN
___ **Up Close and Personal**	0-8217-7956-7	$7.99US/$9.99CAN
___ **Under the Radar**	1-4201-0683-X	$6.99US/$9.99CAN
___ **Razor Sharp**	1-4201-0684-8	$7.99US/$10.99CAN
___ **Yesterday**	1-4201-1494-8	$5.99US/$6.99CAN
___ **Vanishing Act**	1-4201-0685-6	$7.99US/$10.99CAN
___ **Sara's Song**	1-4201-1493-X	$5.99US/$6.99CAN
___ **Deadly Deals**	1-4201-0686-4	$7.99US/$10.99CAN
___ **Game Over**	1-4201-0687-2	$7.99US/$10.99CAN
___ **Sins of Omission**	1-4201-1153-1	$7.99US/$10.99CAN
___ **Sins of the Flesh**	1-4201-1154-X	$7.99US/$10.99CAN
___ **Cross Roads**	1-4201-1192-2	$7.99US/$10.99CAN

Available Wherever Books Are Sold!
Check out our website at **www.kensingtonbooks.com**

More by Bestselling Author
Hannah Howell

More from Bestselling Author
JANET DAILEY

Calder Storm	0-8217-7543-X	$7.99US/$10.99CAN
Close to You	1-4201-1714-9	$5.99US/$6.99CAN
Crazy in Love	1-4201-0303-2	$4.99US/$5.99CAN
Dance With Me	1-4201-2213-4	$5.99US/$6.99CAN
Everything	1-4201-2214-2	$5.99US/$6.99CAN
Forever	1-4201-2215-0	$5.99US/$6.99CAN
Green Calder Grass	0-8217-7222-8	$7.99US/$10.99CAN
Heiress	1-4201-0002-5	$6.99US/$7.99CAN
Lone Calder Star	0-8217-7542-1	$7.99US/$10.99CAN
Lover Man	1-4201-0666-X	$4.99US/$5.99CAN
Masquerade	1-4201-0005-X	$6.99US/$8.99CAN
Mistletoe and Molly	1-4201-0041-6	$6.99US/$9.99CAN
Rivals	1-4201-0003-3	$6.99US/$7.99CAN
Santa in a Stetson	1-4201-0664-3	$6.99US/$9.99CAN
Santa in Montana	1-4201-1474-3	$7.99US/$9.99CAN
Searching for Santa	1-4201-0306-7	$6.99US/$9.99CAN
Something More	0-8217-7544-8	$7.99US/$9.99CAN
Stealing Kisses	1-4201-0304-0	$4.99US/$5.99CAN
Tangled Vines	1-4201-0004-1	$6.99US/$8.99CAN
Texas Kiss	1-4201-0665-1	$4.99US/$5.99CAN
That Loving Feeling	1-4201-1713-0	$5.99US/$6.99CAN
To Santa With Love	1-4201-2073-5	$6.99US/$7.99CAN
When You Kiss Me	1-4201-0667-8	$4.99US/$5.99CAN
Yes, I Do	1-4201-0305-9	$4.99US/$5.99CAN

Available Wherever Books Are Sold!

Check out our website at **www.kensingtonbooks.com.**

31901065370951